After the Táin

After the Táin

A Tale of Cú Chulainn

David Jordan

PRESS

Published by Vulpine Press in the United Kingdom in 2023

ISBN: 978-1-83919-501-3

www.vulpine-press.com

For my mother, Marian Jordan

Thanks to Bryan Jordan, Willie Lynch, Ger Daly

I

Cú Chulainn Loses His Memory and Becomes an Ordinary Man

How did Cú Chulainn forget who he was and, for a time, become an ordinary mortal?

It is soon told.

When Cú Chulainn was a young man, he discovered mead. And like any young man he took great pleasure in it. Of course, Cú Chulainn being Cú Chulainn, he drank at least three times as much as his drinking partners, but he was not immune to its effects, including the inevitable hangover the next morning. Indeed, it is fair to say that he suffered three times as much as his friends did.

Cú Chulainn had many drinking partners but the most steadfast was his charioteer and best friend, Laeg Mac Riangabra. Now, the two friends got into the habit of drinking on the banks of a small river that ran by Emain Macha. In times of peace, they would meet there, most nights, bringing their skins full of mead and their drinking horns.

They talked about many things but mostly women and war. These were, indeed, halcyon days for the Hound.

One evening, Cú Chulainn sat on the bank of the river, waiting for Laeg and sipping mead from his horn. It was in early Autumn. The tall grass he sat in was dry and sweet smelling. Even though the evening was mellow, the birds sang their hearts out. Every now and then he heard a plop from the river as a fish surfaced. Cú Chulainn inhaled deeply through his nose and thought to himself that if he could spend the rest of his life here, drinking in the dim light, listening to the sounds of bird and fish, waiting for his best friend, he would be perfectly happy.

It was a moment.

Cú Chulainn was no longer the beardless youth who had defended Ulster single-handedly from the army of Ailill and Medb. He was now a young man. He had achieved great things and his reputation as Ireland's greatest hero was well established. As mentioned earlier, this was a time of peace but as the Hound sat there, mellowed out, he admitted to himself that he was tired of being Ulster's champion. He was tired of coming home to his wife, blood soaked and depressed after battle and the Warp Spasm. He was tired of being called out by warriors who wanted to gain fame by besting him. He was tired of performing his feats for the boys of Emain Macha. But most of all he was tired of the burden of his destiny: having to die young. So, as he sat there on the banks of the little river, he sighed into the silence.

He heard Laeg coming before he saw him. The charioteer was whistling tunelessly as he approached. Cú Chulainn smiled. His friend had no ear for music. But, even so, it was a sweet sound because he had come to associate it with these blissful hours. Soon, his friend became visible. He strode through the tall, knee brushing grass. A big, blonde, grinning young man. Though he was no musician, he was known for his intelligence and good looks, as well as drinking prowess. And, of course, he was the greatest charioteer in the entire province. He wore a crimson tunic and blue plaid trousers. He had no sword. It was part of the warrior's code not to wear swords whilst drinking. Of course, this left them vulnerable to attack by enemies but it also prevented bloodshed amongst the Ulstermen, drink being often the cause of ire and blood lust, even amongst friends and kin. But there was never any of this between Cú Chulainn and Laeg Mac Riangabra. They found nothing but pleasure in each other's company. It is true what they say. The best things in life are the simple pleasures: drink and conversation by a river as it flowed by.

So, Laeg approached in the falling light as twilight took hold of the world. When he reached Cú Chulainn, he stood there for a few seconds, looking down at the Hound and grinning. Then he fell back onto the grass, seating himself.

'Hello, chief,' Laeg said.

'What are you so happy about?' Cú Chulainn said.

'O, nothing in particular. Life is good. That's all.'

'Yes it is,' Cú Chulainn agreed and took a draught from his drinking horn. 'These are peaceful days,' he said after swallowing the mead and belching.

'Maybe not for much longer, though,' Laeg said. 'Have you heard the news?'

'What news?'

'The Donn Cuailnge is back. He has been spotted in a field near here.'

'So?'

'You know as well as I do what that means.'

'No, I don't. Tell me what it means,' the Hound said.

'It means trouble. Whenever the Brown Bull is around, strife happens.'

'Coincidence.'

'No it isn't. That bull is a curse. Ever since the business with Medb and Ailill of Connacht.'

'Is that why you are so upbeat?' Cú Chulainn said.

'No. I don't relish the prospect of war. But these things are out of our hands. Just enjoy life while you can, right?'

'Damn right,' the Hound said.

'But there is hope that this time it might mean something else. It seems the Brown Bull has found himself a girlfriend,' Laeg said.

'A mate? You're kidding me.'

'No. A great heifer with a multi-coloured coat. Almost like a rainbow, I'm told. She has been spotted in a field close to the Brown Bull.'

4

'Really? So, the old bull has finally succumbed. We all do in the end, I suppose.'

'Yes. And everyone is saying it might be a good omen. Maybe there will be a lasting peace.'

'Hmm. It does sound propitious. I just hope he knows what he's getting himself into,' the Hound said and they both laughed. But Cú Chulainn seemed distant and pensive to Laeg. So, he asked him, 'what ails you, Hound?'

'I've shared with you what is in my heart many times, Laeg. You know what troubles me.'

'You are sad because of your destiny.'

'Yes. I'm sad because of that.'

'Well, maybe you won't have to die young. Now that the Brown Bull has found a girlfriend…'

'You can't argue with destiny, Laeg. You know as well as I do that it won't be long before I'm needed in battle again. Before the Warp Spasm is needed.'

Laeg sighed deeply and said, 'yes, I know.'

'Do you have any idea of how frightening it is, turning into that monstrosity? Do you have any idea of how depressing it is turning back into myself again?'

'It's a high price to pay,' Laeg said, nodding.

'Pay for what, Laeg? Pay for what?'

'Fame, I suppose.'

'Fame? I'll tell you about fame, Laeg. It is shallow. A shallow novelty, and the novelty wears off quickly. Believe me.'

'Adulation?'

'Adulation is like poison, if you want to keep a sane mind.'

'What about your skills? All your battle training feats?'

'I tell you, you soon get tired of that, too. Doing the same tricks over and over again. Like a performing clown.'

'What about the women? Weak for you, all of them.'

'I'll admit, that is something. But all in all, you have to agree, I'm getting a pretty bad deal here,' Cú Chulainn said.

'I know. A lot of guys want to be you, man. I did once. But the more I get to know you the more I am happy to be myself.'

There was a pause, in which a plop could be heard from the river.

'What I wouldn't give to make it all go away. To give up the Hound and become Setanta again,' Cú Chulainn said.

'Setanta?'

'My boyhood name. Before I killed Culann's hound and became the mighty boy warrior of Ulster. You know the story.'

'Do you really mean that? About giving it all up?'

Cú Chulainn turned his head and looked his friend in the eye. 'Yes, I do,' he said. 'But there is no going back. No reversing it. I'm stuck with it. Tough break, huh?'

There was another silence. This time longer and deeper, as both young men fell into introspection.

Soon, they were cloaked in shadows as night claimed the land but the conversation picked up again. They talked about the social life of Emain Macha. They talked about the mad druid, Cathbad. They talked about the King, Conchobar, and his Court. They talked about astrology. About the constellations. They talked about their wives' cooking. About picking blackberries. About fishing. And, inevitably, they talked about drinking. Of these and many other things the two friends talked, all the time replenishing their drinking horns. After a couple of hours had passed, they were well on their way to being intoxicated. It was then that the following exchange happened.

'You know, we're lucky really, me and you,' Laeg said.

'Ha ha. How so?' Cú Chulainn responded.

'Well, we have wives to go home to and...well...you know. That poor bull out there, I bet he hasn't known company for a long, long time.'

'The Brown Bull? Yeah I guess so...but wait. You said he found a mate, didn't you?'

'That's right. But I reckon he's been on his own for so long that he's forgotten...you know...how to go about it. And I tell you another thing.'

'What?'

'I reckon once he's had a good go off her, he won't bother us again and there'll be no more trouble. Poor old Bull.'

'You really think it's a sign? For peace?'

'I do. I think it's history in the making. And you know what? I think we have a part to play in it.'

'What part?'

'Our task is to bring them together. He's probably a bit shy and she's probably a bit nervous. We need to just introduce them and encourage them a bit and then let nature take its course. See?'

'I'm not risking getting gored. Nature can take its course just fine without me. You go ahead with it if you want,' Cú Chulainn said.

'I can't do it single-handedly! Come on, Hound! Don't you want to do your bit for peace?'

'I told you, I'm not gonna risk being gored.'

'You won't have to. You can take care of the Heifer, I'll take care of the bull.'

'What are you undermining my masculinity now?'

'No! Gods, you said you didn't want to risk being gored!'

'Can't you pick someone else?' the Hound said.

'No, because there is no one else I trust.'

Cú Chulainn shook his head and sighed before saying, 'when were you planning on doing it?'

'Now, of course.'

'Now? Are you friggin' crazy? You'll get us both killed.'

'It has to be now, Cú. I can feel it in my veins.'

'So can I. It's called mead.'

'It's now or never, man. Now or never. Do you think I'd have the courage to do this sober?'

Cú Chulainn shook his head and sighed again. 'Ok, I'll do it. Under one condition. No Warp Spasm.'

'Yes!' Laeg said and made a fist.

'Now let me have some more mead. This conversation is sobering me up, fast.'

So, after another hornful of mead, the Hound set out with his friend in search of the Donn Cuailgne. As they traversed the fields, they sang songs, arms around each other's shoulders. They stumbled and fell in the wild grass, laughing, and neither was injured, being watched over by whatever divinity it is that attends to young men when they are drinking.

But they failed to find the Brown Bull or the Heifer.

Cú Chulainn opened his eyes to daylight. He was lying on his side in a field. For a while he stayed that way, hoping that this was just another layer of a dream. When he realised it wasn't, he got up into a seating position. His brain throbbed and ached. He looked around him. He had no recollection of how he had gotten here.

He stood up, carefully, not wishing to aggravate the hangover. He turned 360 degrees but there was no one about. He didn't know where he was, whose field he was in. There was no sign of Laeg but he guessed that he was nearby. He was right. He found his friend in a neighbouring field, lying spread-eagled on his back, fast asleep.

Cú Chulainn kicked him lightly on the ankle. Laeg's eyes opened. He moaned but said nothing. His eyes closed again. Once more, Cú Chulainn kicked him. Laeg moaned again. He opened his eyes and looked at his friend in silence. Then he got up, surprisingly swiftly, and stood there, scratching his blonde head.

'What the hell happened?' the Hound said.

'We went in search of the Brown Bull.'

'Yes, I remember that. But what happened after?'

'I guess we didn't find him,' Laeg said and laughed.

'Where the hell are we?'

'I have no idea,' Laeg said and laughed again.

'This is not funny, Laeg. Emer is going to be livid when I get back home.'

'Yes, so is my Aisling.'

'Let's get out of here and find our way back to the village.'

So, they started for home. They crossed many fields. Cú Chulainn had no idea there were so many in the environs of Emain Macha. Soon it became clear that they were lost and so they hoped for some landmark by which to get their bearings, but none appeared.

'This is ridiculous. There can't be this many fields in Emain Macha,' the Hound said.

'I hope we didn't offend some local deity. I've heard of travellers getting lost in fields after disturbing some god or other. Or sometimes it is out of pure mischief.'

'Thanks, Laeg. I was worried before. Now I really am worried.'

'But it usually only happens at night.'

'That's not much comfort, Laeg. What happens if we are still lost at night fall?'

'You could go into a Warp Spasm,' Laeg said.

'What good would that do?'

'You could let out a howl. People will hear it and come and find us.'

'The Warp Spasm is for battle only. It would most likely scare people away rather than bring them to us. Plus, it makes me feel sick and I feel bad enough as is. So, no Warp Spasm.'

Soon, Cú Chulainn began to thirst. Luckily, he had his skin and horn with him. He poured himself a hornful of mead and drank moderately from it. 'Can I have some of that. I'm out,' Laeg said. So, he gave him the mead skin.

Pretty soon they were both in high spirits again.

'This is like hell,' Cú Chulainn said.

'No. Hell is facing Aisling when I get home.'

'You're afraid of your wife?'

'Yes. Aren't you?' Laeg said.

'Yes. I suppose I am.'

'Wait. I've an idea. If we stay missing for long enough, they might start to worry about us. And they won't be so angry.'

'You'd rather spend another night here in the fields than face your wife?'

'I didn't say that. Besides, you don't know my wife.'

'Let's rest a while,' Cú Chulainn said.

'Yes!' Laeg said. They both fell heavily down on the grass.

They were silent for a time. It was a crisp, autumn day. Every now and then a cow lowed. Cú Chulainn plucked a leaf of grass and applied it to his lips. He blew on it and the sound was like a high pitched trumpet producing one long note.

'That's neat,' Laeg said.

'One of my many feats.'

'You should use that in battle. You know, to scare off the enemy.'

'Yeah I could try,' the Hound said and they both broke out into laughter. He blew on the leaf again, producing that same, long, ludicrous note and they laughed some more. When the laughter had run its course, Cú Chulainn wiped his eyes and said, 'I needed that.'

'Any mead left?' Laeg asked his friend.

'None.'

They remained seated and silent in the grass, sobering up again. Their moods turned anxious, even fearful. They were like two lost boys. Dusk was approaching. All the signs indicated that it would be a calm, mellow evening except for them. However, they were wrong.

Cú Chulainn's eyes were as sharp as razors. Even in the dim light he could make out a white robed figure at the end of the field they were sitting in.

'There is someone at the end of the field,' he said and pointed to the solitary walker.

They got up and ran down the field toward the figure. Laeg hollered a few times. As they got closer, Cú Chulainn perceived more. It was a man. He had a great grey beard and his white hair was so naturally wavy it was almost comical. He wore a dirty white robe, girdled by a yellow rope. His nose was large and aquiline.

'It's Cathbad!' the Hound yelled.

Cathbad was the mad druid of Emain Macha. Of course, like any druid, he was well respected in the community but behind closed doors, people made light of him. His oddness and his eccentricities. His innocence. His strangeness. And Cú Chulainn and his friend were as guilty of this as all the rest. But now they saw him in a different light. His wavy hair took on an almost heroic aspect. As did his great aquiline nose and bushy beard. When they reached him, he frowned at them and said, 'what are you two pups up to?'

'We're trying to get home,' Laeg said, breathing heavily after the sprint.

'You're lost?'

'Yes,' the two young men said in unison.

'Hmmm. It's not just me then,' the druid said and stroked his beard calmly.

'You're lost too?' Cú Chulainn said, exasperated.

'Yes, but I don't worry about it. I always find a way home.'

13

The druid continued to stroke his beard, abstractedly. When it was clear that no more words were forthcoming, Cú Chulainn said, 'what's going on?'

Cathbad looked at him through pale blue eyes. 'It's the Brown Bull's woman. She doesn't want to be found and she has magic to ensure that she isn't. I can find her, though.'

'You've seen her?' Laeg said.

'O yes. I've seen her and talked to her. I've even taken milk from her. From her very teat,' Cathbad said. 'Three teats she has: one for forgetfulness, one for remembrance and one for knowledge.'

The two young men stared at the druid, not knowing what to make of this.

'You don't believe me?' the druid said. 'Come with me and I'll introduce you to her.'

The two young men looked at each other. The Hound shrugged.

'We set out to find her. Last night. But we didn't. We got lost instead,' Laeg explained.

'Is that so?' Cathbad said. 'Come with me, then and you can meet her.'

Cú Chulainn looked at Laeg and the charioteer shrugged.

'Ok,' the Hound said.

So, they followed the druid's slim form as the twilight grew. He walked with a staff in his right hand, his head thrust forward. From his right shoulder there hung a brown leather bag.

As the light dimmed, his form became harder to grasp with the eye, as if he were becoming insubstantial. Cú Chulainn had to resist the urge to reach out and put a hand on his shoulder. But soon, to the Hound's relief, the druid began to hum a tune which kept him within the radar of the two young men. Like Laeg, he had no ear for music. But the Hound was not thinking about aesthetics at that time. As they entered another field, the druid stopped humming and, over his shoulder, sent back the following words.

'I thought it was just me she was hiding from. Because I know the secret of her udder. But it appears that she is hiding from you, too.'

'Why?' Laeg said. 'What would she have to fear from us?'

'Who knows? Maybe she fears the Warped One.'

'Please don't call me that, druid,' the Hound said.

'Or maybe she just doesn't want to be found by anyone at all,' Cathbad said.

'Even the Brown Bull?' Laeg asked.

'Yes, even the Brown Bull.'

'So, you say she has three teats,' Laeg said.

'Yes. One for forgetting, one for remembering and one for knowing.'

'And which one did you drink from?'

'Knowledge, of course! I've been spending the last week or so getting high on her milk,' Cathbad said and laughed a lunatic laugh.

'What's it like?' Laeg asked.

'You can find out if you want. But I think it might be different for everyone. What it comes down to, Laeg, is are you mad enough?'

The two friends looked at each other and smiled. Cú Chulainn shook his head. But they didn't say anything.

The Brown Bull's mate had indeed a coat that was multi-coloured, as Laeg had heard. It was, in fact, what you would call psychedelic. And, like the Brown Bull, she was twice the size of any regular animal of her kind. These things were clear to the two young men, even in the fading twilight. The Heifer seemed to emanate her own light.

'There she is,' Cathbad said, in a tone of wonderment, as they entered her field. 'The Great Heifer.'

In the green stillness and silence, the druid indicated that they should follow him.

When they stood before her, the Heifer seemed completely indifferent to their presence. She just stood there, chewing the cud, like any dumb beast of the field. 'Hello, coloured one,' Cathbad said to her but she just ignored him.

'Observe the udder. Three teats, like I told you,' Cathbad said, excitedly. Then the druid rubbed his hands together vigorously before taking a drinking horn out of his leather bag. He tapped the Heifer's rump with his staff a couple of times before approaching the udder. When he was underneath it, he planted his staff in the ground, and reached a hand up to the teat that was furthest from the Heifer's head. He started to pull on it like any farmer would. When the milk started to come, he held his drinking horn under it and filled it to the brim.

'There we are,' he said as he let go of the teat. He walked out from under the Heifer's belly and faced the two young men. Before they could say anything, he drank the entire contents of the horn down in one go. Then he just stood there, looking at them, a milk beard around his mouth. A belch came out of him that was so long and deep it could have come from the underworld. Then he fell back on the grass, spread-eagled. Cú Chulainn walked over to the druid and looked down at him. Cathbad's eyes were wide-open but it was clear that there was nobody at home.

'He's completely out of it,' the Hound said.

'Madman,' Laeg said. There was a silent, surreal moment before he said, 'Well? Are you going to try it?'

'Try what?'

'The teat, of course!'

'No, I don't think I want to follow him. Wherever he's gone.'

'I mean the other teats! One for forgetting and one for remembering. That's what he said.'

Cú Chulainn continued to look down at the druid in silence.

'Remember what you said?'

The hound nodded but Laeg went on.

'You said you would do anything to become Setanta again. To feel no more the burden you feel. The burden of destiny.'

'I know what I said,' Cú Chulainn answered, slowly. 'And I'd be lying to you if I said I wasn't tempted but…'

'But what?'

Cú Chulainn remained silent. The simple truth was that he was afraid and this he couldn't reveal to Laeg. He could share everything with his friend but this.

The Hound returned to where Laeg was standing.

'You think I should?' he said.

'No. I'm not saying you should or shouldn't. I'm just saying you have a chance now and it might never present itself again.'

'If I do this, I might forget that you are my friend.'

'Well then we'll have to start over again, won't we?' Laeg said and grinned.

Cú Chulainn looked at the Heifer's udder. 'How do we know which one is which? The teats, I mean.'

'Well, he said the teat for knowledge is the third one and the teat for forgetting is the first, so I guess it's the one closest to her head.'

'What about you? Are you going to try one?' the Hound said.

'No. You know me. I'm happy as I am,' Laeg said, smiling.

There was a silence.

'Are you really my friend, Laeg?' the Hound said, slowly and distantly.

'Of course! You know I am! Why would you ask that?'

The Hound didn't answer. He just continued to wrestle with his mind, in silence.

'If you don't like it, you can always drink from the other teat. The one for remembering,' Laeg said.

'I don't want to fry my brains, Laeg,' Cú Chulainn said in the same abstracted tone.

The blonde young man laughed and replied, 'I never thought I'd hear the like of that from you, of all people.'

The Hound smiled and looked at Laeg again. 'Yeah, you're right,' he said. He turned to the Heifer. 'What the hell.' He went under her belly, taking his drinking horn from his belt. Then he reached up for the teat nearest to her head and began to milk it into the horn. The Heifer continued to ignore them.

When he had finished, he asked his friend, 'should I drink it all in one go or in several?'

'I don't know. Maybe in one go if you want to forget everything.'

'Ok, here goes,' the Hound said and drank. After five seconds the horn was empty. The Hound looked at Laeg vacantly and staggered about for a few seconds before collapsing spreadeagled on the ground. Laeg stood there, looking at the two bodies in the grass and scratching his blonde head.

'Damn,' he said.

Cú Chulainn, or Setanta as we should now rightly call him, came to consciousness and opened his eyes. There were two faces looking down at him. One was a blonde haired man with a look of concern on his youthful face. The other was an older man with a great bushy beard and slightly crazed eyes. He was smiling.

'How do you feel?' the younger man asked him.

'I feel fine,' Setanta said. And, indeed, it was very warm and cosy under the blanket that had been placed on him. 'Who are you?'

'We're your friends.'

A woman with red hair and a beautiful, sensitive face moved into his vision. 'And I'm your wife.' She looked at him with kind eyes. 'It's ok. You're going to be alright.'

'Where am I?' Setanta said.

'You're home,' the woman said.

Setanta got up on his elbows and looked around him. He was in a dwelling. There was an opening that let in daylight but not enough to fully chase away the shadows.

'Here, I made this earlier,' the woman said and handed him a warm bowl of gruel.

He accepted the bowl and drank from it. Then, looking from face to face, he said, 'who am I?'

'You're Setanta,' the young man said and smiled.

The woman put a hand on his forehead, a look of concern on her face.

'I wish someone would tell me what the hell is going on here. I don't know any of you people,' Setanta said.

'Shhhh. All in good time. Just rest now,' the woman said.

'Feel like a walk?' the younger man said to him after he had finished the gruel and rested for about half an hour.

'Give him more time, Laeg,' the woman added.

'No, I'm ok. I can walk,' Setanta declared.

'Let's go then.'

Outside, Setanta was met with a riot of sensations. The first thing to strike him was the smell of smoke. He looked about and noticed it rising from the thatched rooves of the houses that were everywhere. Next were the people, who milled about place on the muddy paths between the houses. They wore clothes of many kinds and colours. There was a loud social hum that was punctuated by the odd cry or command or even the snatch of a song. Setanta knew these sensations but, somehow, it was like he was experiencing them for the first time. Like he had only dreamed them before.

The men they passed nodded at Setanta with eyes that expressed a mixture of love and fear. The women looked at him with naked desire in their eyes. The young boys and girls who ran about the place stopped and looked at him, awestruck.

'Why are they looking at me that way?' Setanta asked the young man.

'Walk with me and I'll tell you the whole story. First of all, my name is Laeg and I am your best friend. The woman in the hut was Emer, your wife and the man was Cathbad, the druid.'

And so, Laeg told Setanta everything. By the time he had finished they were walking amongst the trees on the outskirts of the village.

'That's quite a story,' Setanta said.

'You don't believe me?'

'If it wasn't so strange, I wouldn't.'

'That's a thing to say,' Laeg said. After a silence, he asked Setanta, 'What are your thoughts?'

'I'm thinking that there is going to be a hell of a lot of disappointed people when this gets out.'

'True. But it was your decision. You are in charge of your destiny now.' Setanta nodded but didn't say anything. 'And if you want to reverse it, the Heifer is still nearby. Cathbad can take you to her.'

Setanta frowned and shook his head. 'No. I need time to think about this.'

'Take it. Go back to your house. I'm sure Emer can help you with it.'

'No, I want to be alone. I'll stay here amongst the trees for a while.'

'Ok, do you know your way home?' Laeg said.

'I'll find it,' Setanta said, his mind distant. And so Laeg left him.

The next morning, Laeg called round to Setanta's house. He found his friend sitting before a morning fire.

'Hey,' Laeg said.

'Hello,' Setanta replied.

'Where's Emer?'

'Gone out.'

Laeg sighed and sat down near Setanta. 'Did you have a think about things? Like you said you wanted to?' the blonde young man said.

'Yes.'

'And?'

'The more I think about this Cú Chulainn fellow, the less I like him.'

'So, you're going to stick with being Setanta?'

'Yes. I am.'

'Ok, but you should know that word has gotten about that you've lost your memory. In fact, that's part of the reason I came this morning. King Conchobar wants to see you.'

'Why?'

'I expect he wants to know what happened,' Laeg said.

'What if I say no?'

'He is your King, Setanta. Nothing can change that.'

'I expect he wants me to turn back into that lunatic. It's the Warp Spasm he cares for. Not me. Not Cú Chulainn. The Warp Spasm is his great weapon. It's all he's interested in. But I'll not turn back. Not for him. Not for anybody.'

'Will you at least come with me to the Fort? Hear him out?'

'I'll come. But nothing will change my mind.'

That morning, as they walked through the village, Setanta got some strange looks from the people that were about. But what was more telling was the amount of people that ignored him. As if he didn't exist. Which, in a way, he didn't, he reasoned to himself. But it didn't bother him. He felt an inner strength and power that he suspected his former self had never had. Maybe it was something in the Heifer's milk. Or maybe it had just been dormant, all those years.

'You know, Cú Chulainn was no lunatic,' Laeg said. 'He was actually a great guy. Except for when he warped out.'

'Nobody cares about Cú Chulainn but you. All they are interested in is the Warp Spasm and how many men he could decapitate with one blow from his sword whilst riding on a five pronged spear.'

'You're wrong there. He was loved by many. And don't forget, it was his decision to become you. He hated the Warp Spasm more than anybody. He feared it more than any enemy.'

'That does complicate things a bit, I'll admit. But there is nothing you or Conchobar or anyone can say to make me revert back to being that man.'

After this exchange, the two young men fell into silence as they walked. The fort of Emain Macha soon came into view. It was situated on a large hill. They were still some distance from it when Setanta could make out the silhouette of an enormous round house with a great conical thatched roof.

'Is that Conchobar's house?' Setanta asked Laeg.

'No. That is the temple. The King's house is nearby.'

The fort was surrounded by a circular wall, made of wooden posts, and a ditch that ran around inside it. At the entrance, there were two warriors standing guard. They gave Setanta a strange look but let the two young men pass. They crossed an earthen bridge and started to ascend the wooden steps that led to the King's abode.

Conchobar's place was a large round house made of tall, red painted posts and a finely crafted thatched roof, from which smoke escaped. Another couple of guards stood at the entrance. Laeg gave their names and one of the guards disappeared inside the house. After a few seconds, he came back out and indicated with a thumb that they should go inside.

The King sat cross-legged on animal pelts and skins before a fire which was in the centre of the floor of the house. Four great wooden pillars held up the roof. There were three other men sitting around the fire. The King was naked down to his waist and holding a great python as it stretched behind his head. He looked up at the two young men. He saw the fear on their faces.

'Don't worry. She's a pet. A gift from an Ethiopian king,' he said and looked at the python's head with fondness. Then he looked at his two guests again and said, 'please. Sit down.'

He was a lean, bright-eyed young man. He had a brown, silken beard and brown hair which fell down his back in three braids of differing colours. One was yellow, one was green and one was dark red. Much of his skin was painted on. Mostly abstract designs: intricate spirals and curves.

'Welcome, Setanta,' he said as they sat down by the fire, across from the King.

'Thanks.'

'We've heard about what happened.'

'And?' Setanta said.

'Well, I'd be lying if I said I wasn't concerned. We are all concerned.'

'Who is 'we'?' Setanta said.

Laeg elbowed him in the ribs. It was no way to talk to a king, but Conchobar said, 'it's ok, Laeg. *We*, Setanta, is everyone in Emain Macha.'

'You want me to turn back into Cú Chulainn.'

'Yes. But I'm not going to command it. I'm asking you.'

'You don't want Cú Chulainn. You want the Warp Spasm.'

Laeg rolled his eyes at this, but the King merely smiled and said, 'that's not true, Setanta.'

'Ok, what is it you want?' Setanta said.

Conchobar paused to consider this before saying, 'Cú Chulainn was not just a warrior. He was a symbol. For everyone who lives in Emain Macha. A symbol of strength and courage. A symbol that put pride in all our hearts. And he was loved and he was beautiful. But more than this, he was my friend. You ask me, what do I want? Well, as King of Emain Macha, I want the symbol. But as Conchobar, I want my friend back.'

'What about what I want?' Setanta said.

'Well, what do you want?' the King said.

Setanta sighed and said, 'just a boring life. A bit of peace. Maybe learn a trade.'

'You would be happy with such a meagre existence?'

'Yes. I want to get as far away from Cú Chulainn as I can.'

'That will be difficult,' Conchobar said.

'I don't care. I don't want any more part of war and battle and bloodshed. I want to try something…creative.'

'Like what?'

Setanta took some time to consider this. 'A bard!' he said eventually. 'I'd like to become a bard.'

Conchobar stroked his beard in silence. After a while, he nodded and said, 'so be it. Fedlimid here will take you on as an apprentice.' He indicated one of the men who sat around the fire. A scruffy, big bellied fellow with iron grey hair and dark eyes that made him hard to read.

'Fedlimid?' the King said.

'As you wish, my King,' the man said.

'Well? What are you waiting for?'

Fedlimid the bard stood up heavily and placed his palms on the belly of his red tunic. 'Come with me,' he said to Setanta. His voice was powerful but gentle. The young man got up and followed him out of the King's house.

Setanta left the place in silence.

After a while, Conchobar said to Laeg, 'what's your take on all this?'

'I don't know. Give him what he wants, I suppose.'

'Yes. I agree.' Conchobar was now looking at the head of the python again. Admiring her. 'Give him what he wants. He'll come round. Eventually.'

Two days later, Laeg paid a morning visit to Setanta's house, to see his friend. Setanta was seated before a fire, his face soft as he gazed into the flames.

'Hi chief,' Laeg said.

'Hello.'

'Where's Emer?'

Setanta continued to look into the flames as he made the following reply: 'Gone out. She goes out a lot. I don't think she likes me. She says I'm odd. And self-absorbed.'

'She said that?'

Setanta looked at his friend. 'Yes. She did.'

'Ah, well. You know how women are. Never satisfied. If it's not one thing it's the other.'

Setanta nodded and returned his gaze to the fire.

'How are you getting on with Fedlimid?' Laeg said.

Setanta looked up at the blonde young man again and shook his head. 'I quit,' he said.

'What happened?'

'He wanted me to learn the Táin. I asked him if I could learn something else. He suggested the story of how Cú Chulainn trained with Scathach in Alba. I asked him if he had any stories not related to Cú Chulainn. He told me he didn't. "Surely there are other tales," I said. "Stories that take place in peace-time." "Yes, there are but I don't bother with them," he said. "Why not?" I asked. "Because the best stories come from war," he said. "War is dramatic. War is tragic and high spirited," he said. "If you want to tell other stories, you can compose them yourself," he said. "But I can't," I said. "I have no memory. And if I did, I could only talk about being Cú Chulainn." Then he smiled at me. It was a hard kind of smile. And I knew then that Cú Chulainn was his man.'

'That sucks, man,' Laeg said. 'What will you do now?'

'I'm going try my hand at metalsmithing. I want to create beautiful objects. Gob is taking me on as an apprentice.'

'That's great! Gob is a sound guy. He won't let you down.'

'I hope I don't let him down,' Setanta replied.

'Just do what he tells you and you can't go wrong. I'll call again in a couple of days. To see how you are getting on.'

When Laeg called a couple of days later, as promised, he found Setanta at the morning fire again.

'Hey,' Laeg said.

'Hey.'

'Where's Emer?'

'She's out. I don't know where. She's stopped talking to me,' Setanta said calmly, all the time looking into the fire.

'What did you do?'

'I don't know.'

'Well, you know how women are. She'll probably let you know after a while. I wouldn't worry about it.' There was a silence before Laeg said, in a tentative voice, 'so, how is the metalsmithing going?'

'I quit.'

'You quit? Why?'

Setanta looked his friend in the eye and said, 'I chose metalsmithing because I wanted to create beautiful objects. Jewellery and adornments and the like. But when I got to Gob's forge, I looked around and my heart sank because all I could see were instruments of war. Swords, daggers, shields and so forth. But I didn't quit. I didn't complain. I could see that these objects, even though designed for battle and bloodshed, were beautiful. I stuck with it. That first day, I helped Gob to make a handsome shield. It was rectangular and curved. Bronze with a silver boss. Around the boss was a lovely spiral pattern that I could have looked at all day. Even though I had only handed Gob his tools as he created it, I felt like I had put some of myself into it. "What do you think?" Gob asked me when he had finished. "It's beautiful," I said. "Yes, it is. Now go to Lugh's Well and throw it in the water," he said. "Lugh's Well?" I asked. "Yes. Throw it in as a sacrifice to Lugh. For peace and prosperity," he said. "But it's so beautiful," I protested. "Often, beautiful things have to be sacrificed to the gods. So that we can enjoy good days. Happy, prosperous days," he said. "But you put so much work into it," I said. "I don't mind. Some men have to sacrifice a lot more. They have to sacrifice their own blood. Their very lives. On the battlefield," he said. "You are talking about Cú Chulainn," I said. He didn't say anything. He just looked at me with gentle but fixed eyes. So, I went to the well and threw the shield in there. And I didn't return to Gob, as I knew that Cú Chulainn was his man.'

'Man, that is a bummer,' Laeg said. 'What will you do now?'

Setanta sighed and said, 'I've talked to Cathbad about becoming a druid. He said he would take me out tomorrow to assist him and get an idea of what life as a druid is like.'

'Are you serious?' Laeg said.

'Yes. I can't think of what else to do.'

'Ok. I'll call round in a couple of days to see how you are getting on.'

31

When Laeg visited Setanta a couple of days later, he found his friend sitting in the shadows against the wall of the house. The fire had died down to embers.

'Well?' he said.

'Well what?' Setanta said.

'How did it you get on with Cathbad?'

'Not too good. Emer's left me.'

'She's left you?'

'Yes, took all her things and went.'

After considering this for a while, the blonde young man said, 'I expect she'll be back again, Hound. I've lost count of the amount of times Aisling has left me.'

'You said 'Hound'. You know that is not my name anymore.'

'Did I? I'm sorry. So, what happened with Cathbad?'

'He took me glamberry picking. He explained that all Conchobar's men took glamberries before they went into battle, to sharpen their senses. So, he always has a large supply ready. We went to a field and he gave me a basket and told me to start picking. He said that I should ingest berries as I picked them as they were good for the mind and he took them regularly himself to help in his priestly duties. So, I did. After a while, I began to feel sick. "Go home to Emer," he said. "A druid who can't take his glamberries is no druid at all." So, I did. I told her I was feeling sick and why. She put a light hand on my shoulder and sighed but the look on her face was not one of concern. She just looked like she was unimpressed. Even slightly contemptuous. After a while, for some reason, I felt a bit turned on. I moved to kiss her but she turned her face away and I kissed her cheek instead. I bowed my head in dejection. She didn't say anything but she didn't need to. I knew that Cú Chulainn was her man.'

There was a long, troubled silence. 'What now, man?' Laeg asked.

'I guess I turn back into Cú Chulainn. I know where I'm not wanted.'

'I'm sorry, Setanta.'

'Why? You're the only friend I have.'

'I encouraged you to take drink from that bloody teat.'

'It was what I wanted. You were only pointing that out.'

Laeg sighed and said, 'what will you do?'

'Find the Heifer again and take drink from the other teat. The one for remembering,' Setanta said. 'Be honest, Laeg. Do you miss Cú Chulainn too? Do you want him back?'

Laeg looked at the ground and shook his head. After a while, he answered thus: 'yes, I want him back. But I want him to be happy, as well. And I don't think he'll be happy as long as he is divided from you. So, I guess the truth is I want both of you.'

Setanta seemed to consider this before saying, 'I want to talk to Conchobar before I turn back into the Hound. There are some conditions I want to lay down.'

'Like what?'

'You'll see. Come with me now to his house.'

Conchobar was seated as before when Setanta and Laeg entered his house. But unlike the previous occasion, there was no fire, no courtiers and no python. He was wearing a plain grey, woollen shirt and yellow plaid trousers.

'Why are you here?' Conchobar asked, after greetings were exchanged.

'Just letting you know that I intend to bring back the Hound.'

Conchobar's eyes lit up and he repressed a smile.

'But there are conditions.'

'Name them.'

'I realise that the Warp Spasm and Cú Chulainn can't be separated. That you can't have one without the other. So, it would be useless for me to insist that there be no more warping. Also, I know that there is no escaping my fate. But there is freedom within fate, Conchobar. I'll fight for you on the battlefield but other than that, I want complete liberty. To come and go and to do as I please. And you can't command me. Ever. I'll be my own man. Not yours. Not Emer's. My own. Master of myself. These are my conditions.'

'That's quite a compromise. You ask for something that I have never given to anyone. Ever. But I will grant you this freedom. I promise I will never command you, only entreat you. Not as a subject but as a friend.'

Setanta inclined his head respectfully and Conchobar returned the gesture.

Laeg grinned and looked from one man to the other and back again.

'What are you so happy about?' Conchobar asked, smiling himself.

'I'm just glad you've made the deal is all,' Laeg replied.

'And I'll bet you're looking forward to becoming the Hound's sidekick again. Freedom for him means freedom for you as well, after all.'

'I suppose you could look at it that way,' Laeg said.

'Go on. The pair of ye. Bring back the Hound. That's the last command I'll give you, I swear,' Conchobar said. And the two young men got up energetically and left the King's house.

As they strode toward Cathbad's place on the outskirts of Emain Macha, Laeg said, 'did you mean what you said about Emer back there?'

'What did I say?'

'That you would no longer be hers.'

'Yeah, I guess so. She hasn't treated me very well, has she? Besides, it's a trap. What use is being given freedom by a king if you don't have freedom from your wife?'

'That's a good line. Maybe you really *should* have become a bard.'

'Thanks.'

'Gee, I hope you remember all this when you take the milk.'

'You think the milk of remembering will make me forget? I think not.'

'So, you will be Setanta and Cú Chulainn in one?'

'That's the plan.'

When they reached Cathbad's house, Laeg called the druid out. A few moments passed and there was no druid, so Laeg called him out again. A half a minute later Cathbad stuck his head out. He looked a bit cross and a bit crazed. Nothing out of the ordinary. 'What do you two pups want?'

'We're going to the Heifer. Setanta here intends to take milk from the teat of remembering.'

The druid grumbled and pleaded, 'does it have to be now?'

'King's orders,' Laeg said and winked at his friend.

Cathbad withdrew his head. There was a sound of general disorder and chaos from inside the roundhouse. Vessels and utensils being knocked and bandied about and falling to the ground. The mad druid cursed a couple of times. He came out a minute later, with his staff in his right hand and a leather bag hanging from his right shoulder.

As they made their way through the fields, it became clear to the two young men that Cathbad was ignoring Setanta.

'It's probably because of the glamberries. He takes these things to heart,' Laeg whispered to his friend.

'What about the glamberries?'

'You got sick from them, didn't you?'

'Yes. But…'

'You know how crazy he is. Just think nothing of it.'

'Stop whispering, you two!' the druid snapped over his shoulder.

'Why should we? We can whisper if we like,' Setanta protested

'It irritates me.'

'Sorry,' Laeg said.

'Just stop talking.'

If the Heifer was impressive by night she was nothing short of magnificent by day. Her coat shone and sparkled like sea-spray. The psychedelics underneath swirled about very slowly and elegantly. Nobody knew whose hand or eye had painted them except that it must have been an immortal. She seemed bigger, too, by daylight. And her body was perfectly shaped and proportioned. And the noble white head, with eyes like rubies, showing a haughty, bovine indifference.

Cathbad told them to approach slowly and silently. This in spite of the fact that she seemed completely indifferent to their presence. But Setanta didn't want to upset the druid again, so he did what he was told.

When they stood before the Heifer, the druid tapped her rump lightly with his staff and said, 'hello, old girl.' She continued to ignore them, munching on the grass. 'This *amadán* has business with you,' he said, indicating Setanta. 'He wants some of your milk.'

The Heifer grunted and Setanta was not sure if it was an affirmative or a negative or just a coincidence. The druid, however, took it as a 'yes' and said to Setanta, 'proceed.'

So, he took his horn from his belt and approached the animal's udder. He reached for the middle teat and began to milk it. Soon, the milk came squirting out in jets and Setanta put his horn under it. Once it was filled, he walked back to the others. 'Drink it down. All of it,' the druid ordered him. And so he did.

When he had finished, he wiped the milk from his mouth with his sleeve and looked at the others.

'How do you feel?' Cathbad said.

The young man appeared to be unaffected. He shrugged his shoulders and belched. Then, suddenly, a startled look came into his eyes, as if some ghost had slapped him across the cheek. He fell down on the grass, first his bum and then his back. He closed his eyes. After a minute or so, when he opened them again, there was a blissful look on his face.

'Setanta,' the druid said, kneeling over him.

'He's blissed out,' Laeg said.

'I can see that,' the druid hissed.

Setanta closed his eyes again, smiling.

Cathbad put a hand on Setanta's forehead. 'Setanta. Can you hear me?'

There was a long, tense silence. Nobody moved or spoke. Again, the young man opened his eyes but this time they were not Setanta's eyes. They were the powerful and slightly crazed eyes of the Hound. He looked at the two faces above him for an instant. Then he got up swiftly and patted Laeg on the shoulder.

'So, that's that,' he said.

'Is it you, Cú Chulainn?' Laeg said.

'Yes, it's me,' Cú Chulainn answered. He offered his hand to Cathbad. They shook hands and he said, 'thanks, druid.'

'Don't mention it.'

Then he turned around and said to the Heifer, 'thanks, girl.' She grunted and he took this to be an acknowledgement.

'So, that's that,' he said, again. 'Let's head back to Emain Macha.'

'I'm sure a lot of people will be pleased to see you again, Hound,' Cathbad said.

'I hope so,' Cú Chulainn said.

And so, the three of them walked down the autumn field in silence.

After a half a minute or so, Cú Chulainn stopped, suddenly. The other two stopped too and turned to look at him. 'What is it, Hound?' the druid said.

He looked at his companions and said, 'I have to know…I can't help it…I just have to know.'

'Know what?' Laeg said. But Cú Chulainn had turned to walk back up the field.

'What's he up to?' Laeg said to Cathbad.

'He's just being Cú Chulainn,' the druid said, smiling after the Hound. Then he looked at the blonde young man and said, 'he intends to drink from the teat of knowledge.'

So, they walked back up the field toward the Heifer. When they got there, Cú Chulainn was lying supine and spreadeagled on the grass again, his eyes shut, a milk beard around his mouth.

'He's out of it,' Cathbad said.

'Not again,' Laeg complained and shook his head.

'Let's watch over him.'

And so, they sat down by him, and prayed for the safe return of Ulster's finest.

II

Cú Chulainn Learns the Secret of Time Travel

How did Cú Chulainn learn the secret of time travel and the magic of the mind warp?

It is soon told.

When he came to, Cú Chulainn found himself floating about in darkness. It felt and sounded like he was on the sea. He floated on his back and above him a dark, starless sky was rent with lightning bolts. There was no thunder except for the soft boom of waves landing on a shore nearby. He had no great desire to see that shore. He had no great desire to swim to safety. In fact, he had no desire to do anything at all, except float and watch the silent show above him. How tranquillising lightning without thunder was! How beautiful and even playful! He felt himself being dragged down into oblivion again and he tried to resist it as he wanted to stay up and watch the spectacle above. But he couldn't resist for long.

He surfaced again. Once more he was afloat in the water. It rocked him like a mother would a baby. And the lightning above him continued to make playful shapes. Like toys above a child's cradle. Both the sea and lightning seemed to conspire to make him sleep. But he could still hear the relentless noise of waves landing on the sea shore nearby and this kept him awake. He wanted to see that shore. After all, he was here for knowledge, wasn't he? In spite of their best efforts to pull him back under, he managed to turn around and swim.

Cú Chulainn was a fine swimmer and he ploughed through the waves, meeting no real resistance. The sea swelled and heaved him about as if in protest and the lightning flashed around him, now more in anger than in play it seemed, but this was no great trouble to the Hound. He continued to power his way toward the shore and whatever it was the sea was trying to keep him from.

When he made land, instead of falling down prone in exhaustion, as you might expect, the Hound started to walk. There was a forest just beyond the beach above and he felt drawn to it.

The line of trees that marked the edge of the forest was as clean and straight as a razor blade. So, when Cú Chulainn entered it, he suddenly found himself plunged into shadow.

He stopped and turned around. There was nothing but profound darkness. That was when he started to hear the voices.

There were three or four of them and at least one was female. They talked softly and subduedly but he could hear them well enough. He turned and walked in the direction they came from. After a while he became aware of a light source. A flickering light. Someone had got a fire going.

Soon, he found himself in a glade, at the centre of which was a large, hungry fire. But there were no people about. Only the voices.

'Come closer so we can get a better look at you,' the female voice said. So he walked toward the fire.

'That's better. My, you are a fine specimen,' the female voice said.

'I thought he would be bigger, somehow,' a male voice added in a stentorian tone.

'He still has some growing to do,' the female voice said.

'Do you know who we are, boy?' the male voice asked.

Cú Chulainn shook his head.

'We are the voices of the fire. Do you know who you are?'

'I'm Cú Chulainn of Emain Macha.'

'That's right. And you drank from the teat of knowledge, didn't you?'

'Yes, I did,' the Hound said.

'So, what do you want to know?' the male voice said.

'Don't rush him. He only just got here,' the female voice said. 'Are you okay, Cú Chulainn?'

'I'm fine,' the Hound answered.

'There, see? The lad is perfectly fine,' the male voice said. 'Now can we get on with this?' The female sighed but said nothing. 'What do you want to know, Cú Chulainn?' the male voice repeated.

'I don't know.'

'You don't know? You drink the milk of knowledge, you come all this way and you don't know?'

'Give him some time, will you?' the female voice said.

'Yes, give him some time,' a second male voice joined in. His was not so deep and powerful as the first male's voice but it was more melodious.

There was a silence. 'Well?' the first male voice said.

'Who are you?' Cú Chulainn asked, trying to keep his voice as even as possible.

'Well, that's good for a start,' the female voice said.

'Yes, it's a start,' the second male voice declared.

'We are the voices of the fire,' the female voice said.

'I don't understand,' the Hound said.

'You drank from the teat of knowledge didn't you?'

'Yes.'

'So, what do you want to know?'

'I wasn't expecting this.'

'Most people say that. You thought it would be more metaphysical, didn't you?'

'Why are you here?' the Hound said.

'Good. We are here to answer your questions. And to determine if you are ready for the fire.'

'The fire? What does the fire do?'

'It is the fire of knowledge. You must step into it but first we must determine if you are ready for it,' the first male voice said.

'And how do you do that?'

'We assess your questions. If you ask the right questions you will be permitted to step into the fire.'

'Won't it be painful?'

'Yes. Agonising. But only for a moment.'

'What happened to the apple of knowledge?' the Hound said.

'This is not a time for levity, boy. But if you must know, we feel that fire is a far more apt symbol. A fire is bright and hungry. Like the mind, it needs to be fed. Its appetite is endless. What's an apple? A fruit you pluck and eat. There really is no comparison.'

'Ok. So I just ask you guys questions? Is that it?'

'Yes,' the second male said.

'I don't know where to start.'

'You already have.'

'There must be something you've always wanted to know about? Something the druids can't help you with. Something that no one can help you with,' the female said.

Cú Chulainn frowned as he searched and sifted through his mind. He shook his head slowly as if in resignation.

45

'There must be something,' the female said again.

The Hound sighed and said, 'there is something. But it's ridiculous. Only a child's fantasy.'

'Tell us!' the female said.

'I've always wanted to be able to travel through time,' the Hound said. He was met with silence. 'See? I told you it was ridiculous.'

'Questions now, Cú Chulainn,' the female said.

'How do I travel through time?' the Hound asked.

'How would we know?' the first male said.

'Can I travel through time?'

'Yes.'

'What's involved?'

'Magic. Danger.'

'Why danger?'

'All power is dangerous.'

'Where must I go?'

'Into the fire.'

'Ok,' the Hound said and tried to think of more questions. 'Who will show me? I mean, who will teach me?'

'Merlin will.'

'Who's Merlin?'

'A famous druid.'

'More famous than me?'

The female laughed and said, 'in certain parts of the world, at certain periods, yes.' There was a silence as the Hound racked his brains for another question. Something

46

that would be fruitful but also would allow him to maintain his dignity. But all he drew was a blank.

'I can't think of any more questions,' he said at last, suddenly feeling very weary. 'How do I get home from here?'

'You would give up so easily?' the second male said.

'I can't think of any more questions,' the Hound repeated.

'The trick is to be like a child once more. A child of six or seven years. You must question everything and, more importantly, you mustn't be afraid to question. You must be uninhibited,' the female said.

'Are you finished, woman?' the first male said testily. 'You're making it far too easy for him.'

Cú Chulainn sighed and tried to imagine himself as a child of six or seven. What would the boy Setanta say to these disembodied voices?

'Where are your bodies?' he said at last.

'We don't have any,' the female answered.

'What happened?'

'We don't remember,' the second male said.

'Is it scary?'

'No. Not really.'

'Where am I?' the Hound asked.

'You're at the fire of knowledge.'

'Who made the sea and the lightning?'

'The mother and the father of the gods.'

'Why did they make me want to sleep?'

'To keep you safe.'

'From what?'

'The fire, of course.'

'Will I ever see Emain Macha again?'

'Yes.'

'Am I in danger?'

'Yes.'

'How so?'

'We've already told you.'

'What happens after I step into the fire?'

'We don't know.'

'Does everyone come here? Everyone who drinks the milk?'

'Not everyone. Only those who can resist the sea.'

'Did Cathbad come here?'

'Yes, he did.'

'What did he ask for?'

'Confidential.'

'Will I die young?'

'Yes.'

'Why?'

There was a silence before the female said, 'that is something only the fire can answer. Now we must ask you a few questions.'

'Ok.'

'Why do you want to travel through time?'

'I don't know. Adventure, I suppose. And to learn.'

'Where will you go?'

'Firstly, I think I'd like to see Helen of Troy.'

'Why?'

'Because I want to see the most beautiful woman that has ever lived.'

There was another silence before the female said, 'how much do you want this knowledge? Be honest.'

'Well, now that I think of it, I want it more than anything I've ever wanted.'

More silence. 'Hmmm. He sounds genuine enough to me,' the female said. 'I'm happy if you two you are.'

'Yes. I'm happy too,' the second male said.

'You're always happy,' the first male grumbled. 'I'm not so sure about this one. But I won't force a majority rules decision. So, I guess I'm ok with it.'

'Excellent. Cú Chulainn, you may step into the fire. But first, you must collect some sticks to feed it with,' the female said.

'You want me to get you some fire wood?'

'Yes. That is the way with all who approach the fire. Sure, how can we do it ourselves when we have no bodies?'

'Ok,' the Hound said and turned and exited the glade to find some wood.

'Don't be stingy now. A fine strapping young lad like yourself,' the second male called after him.

When he returned with a pile of wood the female said, 'very good, Cú Chulainn. Now, toss them on the flames.'

He did so. 'Now you may step into the fire of knowledge and see what awaits you on the other side.'

'Do I have to step? Can't I run at it and leap? I'd say it would be a lot less painful,' the Hound said.

'It won't make any difference.'

'Still, I'd like to.'

'As you wish.'

So, Cú Chulainn walked back to the edge of the glade and turned around to face the fire. Then he ran at it with all the speed and courage he could muster. When he was a couple of paces away from it he leaped as high and long as his strength would allow. Then all was consumed in searing whiteness.

The pain Cú Chulainn felt on entering the fire was so intense that it would be futile to try to put it into words. But the relief he felt afterwards as he came out of it was equally unfathomable. As is the way with all our kind, he would remember the pain over the pleasure for the rest of his short life.

So, his body tumbled and rolled down over hard ground until it met with something solid and came to a stop. Slowly, he turned his head and looked up. He had expected to see a tree or a rock but no, it was a man. The first thing to strike the Hound was how ugly he was. He had a pug nose and a thick, scruffy beard. His mouth was down-turned and his great, domed head was almost completely bald. But his eyes were kind. The man wore a faded and stained toga. Cú Chulainn got up gingerly until he faced the man. He was a foot taller than him.

'Hello, Lad,' the man said and grinned up at him. He had a fierce grin, the top row of his teeth meeting his bottom lip.

Before he could answer, the Hound felt a stiff breeze brush against his body, making him shiver. He realised he was naked. The fire must have burned off his clothes.

'Here. Put this on,' the man said and handed him something that looked like a blanket. Cú Chulainn took and unfolded it.

'What is it?' the Hound asked.

'It's a toga. Here, I'll help you with it,' the man said.

Once he had the toga on, Cú Chulainn looked down at himself and felt another gust of breeze, cold against his skin. 'It's freezing. How do you stick it?' he said to the man.

'Come now, don't exaggerate. It's not all that bad. Besides, the cold is good for the mind. It's invigorating.'

'Who are you?' the Hound said.

'My name is Socrates.'

'The philosopher? From ancient Greece?'

'That's right!' he said and grinned, making his face more ugly but also, somehow, more endearing.

The Hound looked around him. It was midnight dark and he couldn't make out anything except the stars that peppered the sky.

'Dark again,' he said.

'Does this trouble you?' Socrates said.

'No, it's just that ever since I came here it's been dark.'

'It speaks to the human condition. We're all in the dark. We don't really know anything.'

'I think my old druid, Cathbad, would disagree with you there.'

'Yes, he is a bit arrogant, isn't he?' Socrates said.

'You've met him?'

'Yes. Many times.'

Cú Chulainn frowned at the pug nosed philosopher. 'Who are you? I mean, what do you do here?' he said.

'Me? I'm a guide, of course.'

'To where?'

'You tell me.'

'I was told I had to see a druid named Merlin,' the Hound said.

'Ah. Can I ask why?'

'I want to learn about time travel.'

'I see. Well, he's the man who can help you with that.'

'You've taken others to him?' To learn how to time travel?'

'You wouldn't be the first and you won't be the last. Can I ask you where you want to travel to?'

'I want to see Helen of Troy.'

'Ah, good choice,' Socrates said. 'The face that launched a thousand ships.'

'Have you ever done it? Travelled through time, I mean.'

'O, yes. The technology is widely available. Though not yet to you barbarians. It's easy. You'll see.'

'Ok, well I guess we should be on our way, shouldn't we?' Cú Chulainn said.

'Indeed! Come with me,' the philosopher said and grabbed lightly Cú Chulainn's arm. 'Do you like to talk, lad?'

'As much as the next person.'

'Good. Because I love to. Especially with young people like yourself.'

They took a small path that turned and winded but was never out of earshot of the sea. The night was calm, clear, almost serene. The salt smell of the sea mingled with that of the earth and the aroma of flowers. As they walked, they kept up a constant dialogue, with the philosopher asking most of the questions. Indeed, it shamed Cú Chulainn to admit that the old man was far more hungry for knowledge than he was. Every time he answered one of his questions, the philosopher seemed delighted and spurred on to ask another one. The Hound had never met anyone like him.

After a while, Cú Chulainn began to ask Socrates questions.

'Our druid, Cathbad, holds you in high esteem. He said that you invented philosophy.'

'O, I wouldn't go that far. All I did was ask some questions. Most of the work was done by my successors.'

'He said that you were sentenced to death because you denied the existence of the gods.'

'I didn't deny it. I merely questioned it.'

'My father is a god. Do you question that?'

'Yes, I do.'

'Are you saying I'm a bastard?'

'No. I'll bet you have a mortal father as well. That is often the case with demi-gods.'

'Yes, I do, in fact. His name is Sualdam.'

'There, see?'

'Where do you stand on fate and destiny?'

'I don't know, lad.'

'Come on. You must have something to say on it.'

'No, I really don't,' Socrates said. 'Where do you stand on it?'

'I'm troubled by it,' the Hound admitted. 'My destiny is to die young.'

'Ah, maybe you should seek out Achilles then. You know, after you see Helen of Troy.'

'Why?'

'Well, Achilles was also destined to die young and, like you, he was troubled by it. You are the Irish Achilles.'

'Is that right?' Cú Chulainn said and fell to musing on this. Before long they resumed their conversation.

Socrates was by far the most eloquent man Cú Chulainn had ever met, and he had met a few. Talking with him, against the quiet susurrus of the sea, put him into a kind of mellow trance. His sense of time and distance softened and distorted. The philosopher's energy was boundless and he could almost feel it coming at him in waves. Waves that seemed to harmonize with those of the sea. He was also probably the most cheerful man Cú Chulainn had ever met. The joy he took in the company of the Hound was obvious. And Cú Chulainn's warmth and respect toward him grew with each turn of the path. When it came time for them to part, it was with much regret on both sides.

So, Cú Chulainn came out of his trance to find himself standing before an old round-tower. The light and the bird song indicated that it was early in the morning. There was no sign of Socrates but Cú Chulainn wasn't perturbed by this. By now, he was used to reality shifting on him. He looked up at the tower in admiration. It was about forty meters high, with a conical roof. The door was situated about three metres above the ground and there was a wooden ladder resting against the masonry below it. Just beyond the tower were the ruins of what had once been a large and complex structure.

'Helloooo!' Cú Chulainn called up to the top of the tower, where a window was visible. A half a minute passed and the Hound was just about to call out again when a man's head emerged.

'What is it!' the man yelled.

'Are you Merlin?! The druid?!'

There was a few seconds of silence before the man answered, 'yes!'

'My name is Cú Chulainn! I'm here to learn about time travel!'

'You're Cú Chulainn?!'

'Yes!'

'The Hound of Ulster?!'

'Yes!'

'I find that hard to believe!'

'But I am!'

The man sighed loudly and said, 'Ok, come on up!'

Cú Chulainn walked to the ladder and, climbing it, made the doorway. Inside the tower was another ladder that went up through a wooden ceiling. He climbed up to find yet another ladder and another ceiling. After another two floors, he emerged into the high room of Merlin.

The druid was a raven haired young man, with a Machiavellian countenance. He wore a baggy white shirt and black trousers. His fingers were adorned with rings, some crested and some bejewelled. He sat on a plain wooden chair, his right elbow resting on the back of it. He regarded Cú Chulainn with just a hint of a sneer but the Hound didn't take it personally.

'Have a seat,' he said. Cú Chulainn looked around him. There was a small wooden stool.

'Here?' he said to the druid.

'Yeah, make yourself at home,' Merlin said. 'So, you're the legendary Cú Chulainn. I've heard a lot about you. Do you know who I am?'

'You're Merlin.'

'Do you know what I am?'

'Yeah. A druid.'

'Not just any old druid. I am the last druid.'

'Really?' Cú Chulainn said and made a face.

'You see all these books about you?' Merlin said.

'Is that what they are called?'

'O, yes. I forgot. You wouldn't know what a book is.'

Cú Chulainn shook his head.

'Well, that is something we'll have to remedy then. If you want to learn about time travel.'

'Do you mind?' the Hound said and made to pick up a book.

'Not at all.'

The book had a soft, brown leather cover. Cú Chulainn opened it and thumbed through the pages. 'What is it?' he said.

'It's called writing. And it is the most powerful magic ever invented,' Merlin said. 'It spelled the end for my kind. The druids, that is. In our day, we were the mainspring of knowledge in society. Our trained memories gave us a special status. But when writing was discovered, the need for memory as a repository of knowledge was undermined. In a few short centuries we found ourselves obsolete. Now, I spend all my years sitting up here alone, surrounded by the very magic that put me out of business. Fate has dealt me a strange hand.'

'You say I have to learn this magic in order to time travel?'

'Yes.'

'Socrates said it was a technology. A technology that is widely available,' the Hound said.

'Magic. Technology. They are two sides of the same coin. And yes, more and more people are doing it.'

Cú Chulainn nodded and placed the book back on the stack he had taken it from. 'You must have a lot of knowledge, judging by all these books.'

'I have enough to keep me going,' the druid said and smiled. There was a silence as the two men regarded each other. Eventually, Merlin broke it by saying, 'so, where do you want to travel to?'

'I want to see ancient Troy. You know, during the Trojan war.'

'Ah,' Merlin said and got up from his chair. He went to a pile of books in a corner and started to dismantle it. 'Here we are,' he said and returned to his seat with another leather-bound volume. He opened the book and thumbed through it, stopping randomly at pages. 'Here,' he said and then handed the book to Cú Chulainn.

'What is it?' the Hound said, looking at and feeling the soft, leather cover.

'It's a time machine. Or as close as we'll ever come to one. The book is a translation of Homer's Iliad and Odyssey by George Chapman. If you want to see ancient Troy during the war, you must read the Iliad.'

'This is going to take me some time to learn,' the Hound said, thumbing through the pages.

'That is not all. After you read the book, you must go into a mind warp.'

'A mind warp?'

'Yes. It just means travelling to another place mentally. That is where the real magic happens.'

'So, I just imagine myself to another time and place? Is that it?'

'No, it is more powerful than that. For you at least. You must use the energy of the Warp Spasm. You must channel it into your mind and it will take you to wherever you want to go. All that energy you have. All that power. If you harness it, there's no telling where it will take you.'

'Why does it seem like you were expecting me?'

'Maybe I was. I've read a lot about you. In my time there are a lot of people interested in you.'

'I should hope so!' the Hound said and smiled wryly. 'Will you teach me? About all this reading and mind warping?'

'Of course!'

'How long will it take?'

'A month. Maybe six weeks.'

'I don't know if I have the time, Merlin. They are waiting for me. Back in Emain Macha. I don't know how long it will be before I wake from this.'

'Don't worry about that. There will be time enough.'

'So, what is all this? You, Socrates, the voices of the fire. Is it all just a mind warp, as you call it?'

'Yes and no,' the druid said. There was a silence. Cú Chulainn shook his head. 'Do you want me to expand on that?'

'Please.'

'Yes, in that you are on a mental journey but no, in that there are people and objects here that are beyond your knowing. Like me and this tower. So, I would say that what you are experiencing is more real than a mind warp.'

'I see.'

'Any more questions?' the druid said. The Hound shook his head. 'Ok then, let's get started.'

Cú Chulainn learned fast. After three weeks had passed he was reading the Iliad as well as anyone could. As the old saying goes, he discovered brains he never knew he had. Merlin took genuine pleasure in watching his protégé develop so rapidly. He would get the Hound to read aloud passages from Homer and, if the reading was flawless, which it often was, he would applaud the young man and get up and grab him by the shoulders enthusiastically. Indeed, he proved to be as good a teacher as Cú Chulainn was a student. It is fair to say that a strong bond grew between them and it was as good an example of Platonic love as to be found anywhere.

Merlin had said that, as far as time travel goes, magic and technology were two sides of the same coin. Because Cú Chulainn had a fully mature mind when he began his education with the druid, he had perhaps a better appreciation of writing as a form of magic rather than a science. As the signs on the page began to generate thoughts and images in his head, as they began to transform his consciousness, he became aware of writing as a very powerful art. This is something we miss out on when we are thought how to read and write from a very young age. The mind is so passive during these years that we just accept what we learn without seeing the power and beauty in it. By the end of a month's learning, Cú Chulainn's life was changed irrevocably. His imagination had expanded so dramatically, and his knowledge increased so rapidly that he knew there was no turning back. The idea of time travel, as it was understood by the druid, suddenly became so much more plausible. And the magic of the mind warp became something that was within his grasp.

As instructed, he read mainly the Iliad and the Odyssey of Homer. Aside from being his time travelling destination, the language was so direct and the thought so pure and serene that it was the ideal book to begin his education with. He found himself easily transported to the plain of Troy and the battlefield where the Achaeans and the Trojans slaughtered each other. Indeed, the descriptions of a ruling warrior caste were something that he was very familiar with. He read with interest about the anger of Achilles and his trouble with his fate, keeping in mind that Socrates had described him as the Irish Achilles. And, with more interest, he read about Helen, the cause of the whole Achaean expedition. As Homer gave only a few details about Helen's appearance, the Hound was left to his imagination when summoning up a vision of her in his mind. He found himself impatient to go into the mind warp. Even though he knew he would be conjuring her up from his own dream stuff, he needed to see her as if she were a real person. Cú Chulainn had known many beautiful women in his time. His wife, Emer, was one of them. He had lusted after her greatly when pursuing her and when he had finally got what he wanted he found he enjoyed her company, too. She became like a best friend to him. But Helen of Troy would be different. Her beauty, like the wrath of Achilles, would be something divine and cosmic. He found himself wanting to gaze on that face more and more as his learning advanced. Indeed, it became almost emblematic of that learning. A divine seal of approval, if you will. He felt like his education wouldn't be complete until he had gazed on that face. He told Merlin as much and the druid agreed with him.

'I can't do much more for you. Your mind is your own now and you are free to go where you please with it. If you feel you are ready for the mind warp then you must go ahead with it.'

'Will you help me?'

'Of course! I'll help you to get into the warp and I'll watch over you when you are gone. Remember, you will be very vulnerable.'

'Where will we do it?'

'Wherever you are most comfortable,' Merlin replied.

'There is a tree near here. Where I sometimes go to read. Can we do it there?'

'Yes. I think I know the tree. You wouldn't be the first to read under it.'

'Have you taught them how to warp too? Your other students, I mean?'

'Yes, but you are the first I've taught who possesses the Warp Spasm.'

'What will happen?'

'Well, to be honest, I'm wondering about that myself,' Merlin said and smiled his Machiavellian smile.

'You are in the dark,' the Hound said.

Merlin nodded.

The reading tree, as Cú Chulainn had come to call it, was tall and green and had tremendous girth. He had no idea what species of tree it was. All he knew was that it was perfect for reading under. The roots at the base of the trunk flared out creating four natural seats, one of which the Hound fit into snugly. The foliage above provided just the right amount of shade and birdsong. Sometimes, when it caught a breeze, the tree would sigh and it always seemed to Cú Chulainn not like a sigh of distress but a sigh of pleasure. The seat he sat in faced the ruined complex of buildings associated with the round tower. Merlin had told him about the men who had once lived and worked in those buildings. About the great work they did, wielding the new magic of writing and helping to preserve Irish folklore and mythology. Indeed, he said that neither himself nor Cú Chulainn would probably exist here and now if it wasn't for those men. The Hound tried to get his head around this but it was too difficult to grasp so he gave up. He preferred to just sit and contemplate the ivied remains of the monastery. They made him feel peaceful and intimated to him that the end of all things need not be sad or woeful. Indeed, they made him feel like all was right with the universe.

III

Cú Chulainn Visits Ancient Troy

How did Cú Chulainn travel to the Trojan War and fight with the Achaean Champion, Achilles?

It is soon told.

Once Cú Chulainn was seated at the base of the tree and Merlin had placed himself, cross-legged, beside him, they prepared for the mind warp. The druid used a technique that was really quite similar to meditation. He told the Hound to picture a scene from the Iliad and to try to hold it in his mind. Cú Chulainn envisioned a battle scene with two warriors, a Greek and a Trojan, in combat. As is natural, the picture kept slipping out of Cú Chulainn's consciousness but each time he returned to it, he managed to hold it a little longer. After a while, the world around Cú Chulainn began to darken but the picture he held in his mind became brighter and brighter until it was as if a raw midday sun beat down on the two warriors.

Merlin's voice, now distant, continued to instruct him.

'Good. Very good. Now you must summon the Warp Spasm. You must access its energy and channel it into your mind,' the druid said.

'How?' the Hound said and even his own voice sounded distant.

'Where are you?'

'On the battlefield,' the Hound said.

There was a pause as Merlin considered what to do next. 'You must imagine yourself going into the Warp Spasm, but your hands and feet have been bound in chains. All that energy you need to release. You can't release it. Except into the mind. There is no place else for it to go to.'

The Hound did as he was told. The scene before him continued to brighten until it was almost dazzling. He had never been under such a powerful sun. Soon, his other senses became alive to this new reality: he smelled bloodshed, heard the din of weapons and shields clashing, tasted the dust being raised by the fighting combatants. All of these things helped him to summon the Warp Spasm but he stayed restrained, as Merlin had told him to. Though it was hard. He could feel the Warp Spasm raging in his blood, demanding to be set free. He didn't know how long he could keep it bound.

'What do I do now?' he asked the druid.

Merlin sounded very distant. He could just make out his words. 'Keep it chained. For as long as you can.'

'But it's hard.'

66

If there were any more words from the druid, Cú Chulainn didn't hear them. The roar of battle prevented it.

So, he struggled with the Warp Spasm. His body twisted and writhed as it fought the chains his mind had imposed on it.

The battle raging before him flared up into an all-consuming white fire. The brightness became so powerful that it hurt his eyeballs. He feared for his eyesight. He cried out loud but nobody could hear him. How could they when he couldn't even hear himself?

But suddenly, the din of combat died down and the blazing battlefield receded. It was replaced by a vision of a single warrior. He had a horse hair plumed helmet that nodded menacingly as he walked toward the Hound. His bronze armour flashed in the sun, as did his eyes – the man was obviously insane. In his right hand he held two spears and in his left a huge, circular shield. The shield was wrought of such a magic that the Hound couldn't grasp it in its entirety even though physically it wasn't the biggest shield he had ever seen. The warrior stopped a few metres from Cú Chulainn and said two words, and although he spoke them in not much more than a murmur, the Hound heard him clearly enough.

'My time.'

Cú Chulainn had a couple of seconds to register that this was Achilles before everything seemed to blow up. He felt the chains that held back the Warp Spasm explode and a surge of energy passed up through him as he went into his fearsome battle mode. Then he was amidst the slaughter and the fray.

If you've heard me describe the Warp Spasm of Cú Chulainn before, you know what a monstrosity it is. Think of how those warriors, Achaean and Trojan, must have felt on seeing this abomination suddenly appear in their midst. Here, in case you don't know, is a brief description of that terrible transformation. First, his body shook with fury, like a raging fist. Then his limbs shot out lightning fast, so that he stood at least ten feet tall. His legs twisted around so that they were like those of a dinosaur. The muscles around his arms and shoulders bulged and multiplied and sprouted red, bristly tufts of hair. His face grew enormous, with one eye squinting profoundly and the other lolling out to brush against his cheek. And from his head there spouted a black fountain of hot blood that hissed as it ran down his contorted features. But probably worst of all was the beat of his heart which boomed and shook the ground underneath him. It was this awesome spectacle that terrified the soldiers most of all.

So this was how Cú Chulainn appeared on the battleground that lay between the walls of Troy and the beached ships of the Achaeans. But how did the battle appear to Cú Chulainn? He was amazed to find that his mind was as clear and lucid as ever. Normally, the Warp Spasm consumed his mind in its fury and battle lust: he would come out of it with no recollection of his actions on the battlefield. But now he felt very much present and aware of everything that was happening around him. It was like his mind and body had been separated but not severed. He realised that both his mind and body were warping at the same time. He had been transported to the Trojan war using the energy of the Warp Spasm but, it seemed, the Warp Spasm had also been transported.

His first instinct was to come out of the Warp Spasm as he didn't want to injure any of the soldiers that surrounded him. This was not his war. But he knew that if he did so, he would likely be slain. Plus, he didn't even know if he could transform back to his normal state. So, he reckoned his best bet was to run away from the battle ground.

The Achaean and Trojan warriors were coming out of their shock and horror at seeing the Warped One in their midst. Battle instincts reasserted themselves and they aimed and threw their spears at the monstrosity. Cú Chulainn brushed aside the spears as they flew at him. The ones that got through hurt him like hail stones. When their spears had been spent, the warriors stood around the Hound in a rough circle, watching him, silent and alert. No man was brave enough to take on the Warped One in one to one combat. The Achaean soldiers wished that Achilles was here and, though he was their great opponent, so did the Trojan soldiers because they knew that Achilles was the only man able enough and crazy enough to take on this monster from the depths of Hades. But Achilles was not here.

Cú Chulainn attempted to plead with the soldiers, to let them know that he meant them no harm but all that came out of his throat was a kind of guttural groaning sound. So, with no other options left to him, the Hound did something he had never done in his life: he ran away from the battle. First he turned and oriented himself. He wanted to get to the city of Troy, where he could come out of the Warp Spasm safely. Through the battle dust and heat haze, he managed to pick out the walls of the city in the distance. Then, letting out a great bellow, to scare off the soldiers before him and create a pathway, he charged out of the battle arena, his dinosaur legs giving him tremendous swiftness and power. The noise of his feet as they pounded the ground was loud and terrible to hear and the dust cloud that arose in their wake was greater than any the warriors of Greece and Troy had whipped up in their battle frenzies.

Cú Chulainn soon approached the walls of the great city. He stopped for a few seconds to check behind him and when he was sure that nobody pursued him, he came out of the Warp Spasm. But he continued to run. He noticed there were watchtowers on the walls, so he would have been spotted by the guards there but he wanted to enter the city quietly and unofficially, so he ran past the gates and round the city until he was out of sight of the watchtowers. His plan was to leap the wall and drop into the city unannounced.

He estimated that the city's walls were about 25 feet high, no mean feat, but he managed to get on top of them with one mighty salmon leap. While he was there, he had a good look at the city. Cú Chulainn wasn't a well-travelled man but instantly he saw a resemblance to his own Emain Macha: a great bustling town that surrounded a large citadel on a hill.

He dropped soundly into the city. Luckily, he landed in a place that was quiet and shady. He looked around him avidly. There wasn't much to see as his view was blocked by the mudbrick dwellings that he found himself among. He looked down at himself and saw that, yet again, he was naked. The monk's habit Merlin had given him must have been incinerated during the mind warp. So, his first priority was to find some clothes. He didn't have to search for long. He came across an old man sleeping in an alley way, a blanket wrapped around him. The Hound gently pulled the blanket free, smelling the wine off the old man's breath. He wrapped the blanket around his lower body, securing it at the waist. Then he removed a golden armlet from his right upper arm and placed it in the hand of the old man.

Again, Cú Chulainn was not a well-travelled man but this did not mean that he was naïve. He knew that he would stand out amidst the populace. His hair and complexion alone would mark him out as an alien. So, he knew that very soon he would likely have to face some serious questions and, therefore, he would have to have some answers ready.

He would have to have a story. Whether this was going to be a genuine story or a contrived one, he now had to decide. He asked himself why was he here? The answer was, of course, to look on the face of Helen of Troy. She would most likely be found in the palace on the hill at the centre of the city. So, that was his destination. As to his story, he could not think of any that would likely convince King Priam to let him see this woman, so he reckoned it was best to be honest.

As already mentioned, Cú Chulainn knew that he would stand out amid the Trojans. But he was surprised by just how much this proved to be the case. Almost everyone he passed stared at him, some with wonder, some with fear and some with outright hostility. Of course, his physical appearance must have accounted for much of this reaction but he also reasoned that it was a time of war and in such times suspicion is rife. Nobody approached him. Not even the battle weary soldiers he passed. Though he was unarmed, he went on his way unchallenged. Slowly and deliberately he ascended the terraces toward the citadel. When he came within view of the great portico of the palace, he saw a tall man in a white robe standing on the floor of the entrance, surrounded by guards. It seemed word of his presence had preceded him.

He stopped at the bottom of the steps that ran up to the portico. Priam was a very tall and broad shouldered man in early old age. His white beard and hair were thick and curled and the eyes that gazed out between them were of the lightest, cerulean blue, visible even from where the Hound stood. He smiled at Cú Chulainn and beckoned him to climb up the steps. When he stood before Priam, the King looked at him with a species of awe in his eyes. He looked at the Hound's face in this way for fully half a minute before murmuring, 'so, it is true what they say.'

'What do they say?' Cú Chulainn said.

Priam smiled and patted the hound on one tattooed shoulder. 'What is your name, son?' he asked.

'I'm called by many names. You can call me Hound. And you are King Priam?'

'Yes, I am he. Welcome to our city,' Priam said and held his hand out for Cú Chulainn to shake. Once this had been done, the King introduced a slim, young man who stood nearby. He was dressed in a handsome bronze breastplate and was holding a plumed helmet in his left hand. He had the same eyes as the King and in them was the same species of awe. 'My son, Paris,' Priam said and Cú Chulainn shook the young man's hand. Then, formalities over with, Priam asked the Hound to follow him into the palace.

Once more, Cú Chulainn was reminded of Emain Macha. The main hall was a huge, rectangular space with four pillars holding the roof up and a giant hearth at its centre, in which a fire blazed and danced. Priam sat on a spare, wooden throne beyond the fire. There was a strong spicy odour in the air that Cú Chulainn had never smelled before but it agreed with him.

'So, Hound. Tell us. Where do you come from? And why do you visit us in these troubled times?'

Cú Chulainn cleared his throat and said, 'I come from a land far north of here. We call it Eriú or Ireland. And I come here to look on the face that launched a thousand ships. The face of Helen of Troy.'

There was a silence as Priam exchanged a long meaningful look with his son. 'You've heard of us? The war?' he said, at last.

'O, yes. It is the war to end all wars. How wouldn't we?' Cú Chulainn spoke, tactfully.

'And whose side are you on?'

'I am on no side. This is not my war,' the Hound said.

'So, you've come all this way just to look at the woman my son here stole from King Menelaus?'

'Yes. Her beauty is legendary where I come from.'

Priam regarded the Hound for a few seconds, his bearded cheek resting against the palm of a hand. 'Tell me more of this land you come from,' he said.

Cú Chulainn sighed and said, 'it is not very different from this city you rule over. We, too, have a king who rules from a palace. I have fought many battles for him.'

Priam nodded and said, 'are all of you so spare of speech?'

'Not at all,' Cú Chulainn said. 'We are well known for our eloquence. It's just not something I was bestowed with when I was conceived.'

'So, you are a warrior?'

'Yes. I am.'

'Do you have a woman?'

'Yes, I do.'

'Ah, see my son here,' Priam said and indicated Paris. 'He has a weakness for them. Started this whole bloody business off, didn't you?' Paris frowned and shook his head but said nothing. 'If he could fight as well as he seduces, we'd have ended this war a long time ago.' There was another silence before Priam said, 'are you alone?'

'Yes.'

'How did you get here?'

'A secret way,' the Hound said.

'A secret way?'

'It involves magic.'

'I see,' Priam said. 'Do you have priests where you come from?'

'Yes but we call them druids.'

'So, you have gods?'

'Yes.'

'Tell me about your gods, Hound,' Priam said.

Cú Chulainn sighed again and said, 'well there is the Dagda, who is the father of all the gods, and his son, Lugh, who is the god of light and reason and...' So, he listed all the gods and goddesses of the Irish pantheon and all their functions and provinces, and how they are inter-related. When he had finished there was yet another silence. Priam had closed his cerulean eyes and appeared to be dozing.

'Father?' Paris said. The old man didn't stir. 'Father!' Paris said with more force.

The King awoke with a nervous jerk and looked around him. When his eyes rested on Cú Chulainn again, he said, 'I'm sorry. So you wish to look on the face of Helen of Troy. I will grant you this boon but only if you agree to one thing. Fight for us!'

'That I cannot do. This is not my war.'

'Well, then, go home,' the King said and smiled and raised his palms outwards.

Just then, there was a bustle and a terse exchange of words at the entrance to the hall. Cú Chulainn turned around and saw a single Trojan warrior striding toward them, his helmet in his hand. When he stood before them, Cú Chulainn knew that this must be Hector, the champion of Troy. His face was dark and sweated from battle. His brown eyes were fierce. Dust clung to his massive arms.

'Who is this?' he demanded, looking Cú Chulainn in the eye.

'This is Hound. He comes from a land far north of here. Called Eriú,' Priam said. 'He wants to see Helen of Troy.'

'Has this anything to do with the monster that appeared on the battleground today?'

76

'What monster?' Priam said.

'A malformed giant. I am told he appeared out of the blue and attacked our soldiers before running away.'

'Do you know anything about this, Hound?' Priam said.

'I know this monster. It is under my power. It ran away because it didn't want to harm your soldiers. Like I said, this is not our war,' the Hound said.

'Why would you bring such a terrible thing with you to my city?'

'I am bound to this creature and he to me. I am sorry if it upset your soldiers.'

Hector was now looking at Cú Chulainn closely. 'You say you want to see our Helen?'

'He means to steal her from me! Him and his monster from Hades!' Paris interjected, hotly.

'That is not true. I only want to look on one of the wonders of this world. The face of Helen of Troy. That is all. Then me and this creature will leave you,' the Hound said.

'You say this creature is under your power? Does that mean you can control it?' Hector said.

'Yes.'

'Then let it fight for us! If the reports are true then we could win this war in a matter of days, if we unleash this on the enemy,' Hector said.

Cú Chulainn smiled. 'That is a high price to pay for a look at a woman's face,' he said.

'If you win this war for us you can have her. Take her back to this land you came from,' Hector said.

'You would hand Helen over to this Barbarian!' Paris shouted. 'Over my dead body,' he said and drew his sword from its sheath.

'Paris!' the King yelled. 'Put away your sword!' Once the young man had obeyed him, King Priam turned to Cú Chulainn again and said, 'you will see for yourself the face of her that is the cause of all our strife. After that, you will do as you please.'

'Thank you,' Cú Chulainn said and bowed his head respectfully.

So, the Hound followed Priam's two sons to the private quarters of Helen.

She was seated on a cushioned armchair, her feet on a stool, painting her toenails.

'Helen!' Hector interrupted her. She looked up at the three men. 'A visitor. From a land far north of here. He wishes to see you.' She continued to look at them for a few seconds before she put aside the brush and the little bottle of varnish and stood up, smoothing her gown with her hands. She walked over to them, her head high and her shoulders squared. She walked slowly and deliberately until she stood before Cú Chulainn.

After gazing his fill of her, the Hound said, 'I should have known.'

'Known what?' Helen said, quietly.

'I've come all this way, crossed oceans of time and space, to see the most beautiful woman who ever lived, only to find an Irishwoman.'

Helen smiled and, indeed, she was a Celt if there ever was one. Her skin was pale as milk and her hair was long and auburn and flowing. Her eyes were hazel-green, her cheeks were high and prominent and her lips a perfect bow. But it was her smile that really gave her away. Her cheeks rounded up like fresh apples, her lips had just the slightest turn of wryness to them and her eyes danced in an almost roguish way. She may not have been the most beautiful woman who ever lived but she was certainly the most beautiful woman the Hound had ever seen. He drank in the sight of her and before long he understood why he had gotten such strange looks from everyone – the people of Troy, the soldiers, King Priam and his sons. Helen looked just like him! She could have been his twin! All of his features were matched and feminised in her. Helen, meanwhile, had put a palm to his cheek and the eyes that looked up at him were astonished. He knew, when he looked into those eyes, that she, too, saw the uncanny resemblance.

He felt a hand fall on his shoulder. He didn't know whose hand it was but he heard Hector say, 'fight for us, Hound! Fight for us and she is yours!'

'I can't. This is not my war. This is not my woman,' Cú Chulainn said, without taking his eyes off Helen.

'What's this about?' Helen asked.

'They're offering you to me if I fight for them. Me and this beast I own,' the Hound said.

'Ah, I see,' Helen said and, taking her hand from Cú Chulainn's cheek, she turned around and walked across the room to a window that looked out on the city. Again, she walked in a slow, almost stately manner and the Hound had the chance to appreciate her impressive figure. 'So, I am to be treated like a possession again,' she said, disconsolately. 'It doesn't surprise me. Such are the ways of men.'

'Not where I come from,' Cú Chulainn said. 'Women are respected and empowered in my country.'

'Really? Then maybe you should take me. Take me away from all this death. And guilt. I can't stand it anymore.'

'I can't. As much as I'd like to. I came here alone and I have to leave alone.'

'What about this beast you own?' she said.

Cú Chulainn turned around and found that Hector and Paris had left them. So, he talked more freely. 'The beast is part of me. It's called a Warp Spasm. It is my battle mode.'

'Why alone?'

'Because it's just the way things are,' the Hound said. 'Please, Helen, can I look on your face again?'

She turned around and faced him but she remained where she was. 'O, it's just a face. It's not like I'm a freak or anything,' she said.

'Do you believe in love at first sight?' Cú Chulainn asked.

Helen moved to the chair she had been sitting on, her face bowed. When she reached it she put a hand on the back rest and looked up at the Hound. 'Do you love me?' she said.

'Yeah, I think I do.'

Helen sighed and said, 'tell me what you feel, not what you think.'

'I love you.'

'Do you know how many men have said that to me? Why should I treat you any different?'

'Because you feel it too. Don't deny it,' Cú Chulainn said.

Helen moved from the chair to Cú Chulainn again. She put a palm to his cheek once more and looked into his eyes. 'We are total strangers and yet I feel like I've known you all my life. The truth is I'm scared,' she said.

'Of what?'

'Of love. If you go into battle for me, you will likely die. And enough blood has been spilt on account of me. This face. This goddamned face. Sometimes I wish I had been born a wench.'

'I sometimes feel that way about the Warp Spasm.'

'Guilt?'

'Yes!'

'It couldn't match the guilt that I feel,' Helen said.

'Yes, it could.'

'What's your name again?' Helen asked.

'Cú Chulainn is my name.'

'Cú Chulainn, go home now. Forget about me. This city and its troubles. Find yourself a wife and settle down. Live a quiet, boring life.'

'Priam is right. I could end this war,' the Hound said.

'No, don't say that. Don't even think about it. You will be slaughtered.'

'No. Not with my Warp Spasm.'

'Really?'

'Really.'

'Can I see it?'

'Not now. Not here. It's too big. Besides I don't want to frighten you.'

'I'm a big girl.'

'Trust me. You don't want to see it. Not yet.'

Helen sighed and said, 'okay.' She turned away from the Hound again and sat down on the armchair, an abstracted look on her face. 'If you really want to end this war, you must end Achilles. Without him, the Achaeans will lose heart and turn around and go home.'

Cú Chulainn remembered what Socrates had said about seeking out Achilles. The 'Irish Achilles' wasn't it, he had called him? A great warrior of divine parentage who was also troubled by his fate. 'I will meet with Achilles. Where can I find him?' the Hound said.

'At the beached ships of the Achaeans, more than likely. He has had an argument with the Greek commander, King Agamemnon, which keeps him out of the war. The

Achaeans are waiting for him to stop sulking in his tent and enter the battlefield, once again. It is this hope that keeps their campaign alive. Destroy Achilles and you will take the heart out of the Achaeans.'

The Hound nodded. 'I will meet with Achilles. If he is as great as you say he is, maybe we can work out a way to end this war, peacefully,' he said.

Having heard stories of the Trojan war from when he was growing up and having read the Iliad a number of times, Cú Chulainn knew well how things were supposed to work out. Hector kills Achilles' best friend Patroclus and this draws Achilles into battle. He calls out Hector and kills him. Achilles himself is slain by an arrow from the bow of Paris, later on in the war, after the events in the Iliad have taken place. Eventually, through the cunning of Odysseus and his wooden horse, the Achaeans overrun the city and have the victory. Now, the Hound was faced with the prospect of changing history. His intervention might radically change the course of events, leading to another Iliad and a completely different end to the Trojan war.

So, why intervene?

He had come here to look on the face of Helen of Troy and this he had done. So, why not go home? Well, the truth was, he didn't know how to *get* home. How to get back to Merlin and his round tower. Back to the reading tree. So, he reckoned he had more things to do here. More business to take care of. And he knew that, somehow, it involved meeting with Achilles. Maybe he would help to make a peace here and then he would wake up from the mind warp. But he was also forced to question the reality of what was taking place. If it was all in his mind, then he could do pretty much what he wanted to, without it affecting history or legend. But if this was the case, what was the purpose of going into the mind warp in the first place? He had come here for knowledge. If it was all in his head then what knowledge could be had? He had already seen that Helen was just like an Irishwoman.

Cú Chulainn was greatly vexed by these questions.

He stayed as a guest in Priam's palace, everyone hoping that he would enter the war on the Trojan side. He knew that he didn't have much time. Soon, Patroclus would be killed and Achilles would call out Hector and this would be the time to intervene. He would need to act decisively. But did he even have a choice in the matter? Maybe it was all just another part of his damned destiny.

While he waited for Achilles to enter the battlefield, Cú Chulainn spent much of his time in Helen's quarters. This didn't do anything for his relations with Paris, but he felt a strong bond of love with her that went beyond the physical. She reminded him of home. Often he would gaze out the window of her room, at the city below and the guards walking along its walls, his mind on the terrible war that was just out of sight. Helen would walk over to him, put a hand on his shoulder and tell him to come to bed. But he refused. Sometimes, he cursed the woman in his mind for making him feel like he was fighting a war with himself. With his desire. Hadn't he fought enough wars in his life? Wasn't there enough war here in Troy for him?

Because nobody knew of his intentions regarding Achilles, he was not kept up to date concerning the progress of the war. Though they had not given up hope that he would enter the war on their side, the truth was that he was on the periphery of the minds of Priam, Hector and his councillors. But when Achilles did enter the battlefield, he saw and heard the signs. The gates of Troy opened wide and a great dust cloud was raised as its army thundered back into the town out of fear of Achilles. Following this there was a silence. An absolute silence and stillness. As if the city had turned into a graveyard. Cú Chulainn became conscious of his breathing and heartbeat, and his mouth dried up. His time approached. Once more, he felt Helen's hand on his shoulder.

'Come to bed,' she whispered.

He turned around and faced her. By the look of fear on her face he knew that she too had interpreted the signs. Achilles had returned to the battlefield.

'Come to bed, please!' she whispered again.

The Hound shook his head. 'No. It's time.'

'He'll kill you.'

'You should have more faith in my battle prowess, woman. Anyway, I don't intend to fight with him. I just want to talk to him.'

'Achilles is a madman. He won't listen to you. All he understands is violence.'

'That remains to be seen. If what you say is true then I will slay him. Either way, I'm going to end this war.'

'The only person who can end this war is me. I must return to my husband, Menelaus,' Helen said.

'Menelaus will probably kill you. Anyway, do you think Priam and his sons will let you go back?'

Helen looked down at the floor and shook her head.

'Now is my time to intervene,' the Hound said.

She looked up at him again. Looked into his eyes. 'Please, come to bed, Cú Chulainn,' she said.

'Don't do this, Helen.'

At that moment, from beyond the walls of Troy, there came a great bellow. 'Hector!!'

'Achilles is calling Hector out to face him. I must go,' the Hound said.

Helen wrapped her arms around him and spoke into his ear. 'Let Hector meet him. Why does it have to be you?'

'It's my destiny. Let me go, woman.'

'Hector!!' Achilles roared again.

'You will die if you go.'

'That may be so. But I'm not planning on it.'

'Please! I'll do anything. Anything you want!'

'Stop it, Helen.'

'Will I ever see you again?' Helen said.

'Probably not.'

Helen heaved a great sigh and, freeing him from her embrace, she turned around and walked to the bed. She stood over it, her back to him, her arms folded.

'Hector!!' Achilles bellowed once more.

Not knowing what to say, Cú Chulainn strode out of the room but before he was outside, he took one last look at Helen and, deep in his heart, he cursed Achilles.

Cú Chulainn entered Priam's throne room to find Hector sitting by the fire, clearly exhausted. His wife, Andromache, was on her knees beside him, caressing with a slender hand one of his great, dust covered arms. Priam and Paris stood, looking down at them, helpless.

'Hector!!' Achilles called once more from beyond the gates. It began to sound like he was bellowing out of a hellish abyss.

Hector looked up at the Hound. 'What do you want?' the Trojan champion said.

'I'm going to meet Achilles. On the battleground.'

Hector laughed grimly and said, 'come to steal me of my glory? No way, Hound.'

But Andromache turned to look up at Cú Chulainn, hope kindling in her eyes. 'Yes! Let the Hound face him!' she said.

'He had his chance. We could have won this war weeks ago if he had joined us in battle,' Hector said.

'I'm going to meet Achilles outside and I'm going to end this war. Peacefully.'

Hector laughed again and shook his head. 'No you won't. I'll not be branded a coward. I will face Achilles.'

'But you have fought bravely, my son,' Priam said. 'For years you have been our champion. Let him meet Achilles, if he wants to. No one will call you a coward.'

'Have you so little faith in my ability, father? You know, I might actually win,' Hector said.

Priam looked down at the floor and said nothing.

'I see. And what about you, brother? Have you no faith in me either?' Hector said to Paris.

'You have done enough, Hector. You are tired and battle-weary. He is fresh. Let him face that madman.'

'You don't think I've a hope in hell! None of you!' Hector cried.

'If it was anyone else, Hector. But you know that that man is a machine. A man-killing machine. Nobody can defeat him. Except maybe Hound here. And his war beast, that we have yet to see,' Priam said.

'There will be no beast outside when I meet Achilles today. I will confront him, man to man,' Cú Chulainn said.

'Then you will die,' Hector said, matter-of-factly.

'I'm not afraid of death. But I'm also not afraid of Achilles.'

'Then you will certainly die,' Hector said and smiled without humour.

'Hector!!' Achilles bellowed once more.

'This won't be the first time I've entered a battlefield, you know,' the Hound said.

'But it will be the last,' Hector said.

'I don't think so. Haven't you ever heard of the luck of the underdog?'

Hector shook his head and, taking off his helmet, he considered the Hound in silence for few seconds before saying, 'Go then. You are mad. Both of you are mad. You deserve each other.'

Now it was Cú Chulainn's turn to smile grimly but he said nothing.

'Arms!' Priam cried. 'The Hound needs arms!'

'All I need is a sword and shield,' Cú Chulainn said.

'What about a Helmet? Breastplate?' Priam said.

'I prefer to stay light.'

'You would go into battle with nothing more than a shirt and a kilt?' Priam said.

'I've gone in with less,' the Hound said and grinned.

'Maybe you really are crazy,' the King muttered.

Hector tossed him his sword. 'Take this. There is no finer blade in Troy,' he said. Then he tossed him his shield as well. 'Wherever the sword goes, the shield follows. Good luck, Hound,' he said.

Andromache, a dark, complexioned beauty, diminutive in stature, approached the Hound and putting her hands on his upper arms, she stood on her toes and kissed both his cheeks. Then she looked into his eyes and murmured, 'may the gods shine on you this day, Hound.'

Once outside, Cú Chulainn strode purposefully through the streets of Troy, down its tiers, toward the front gate. As he did so, he was joined by curious onlookers, as well as those who had heard rumour of him and his intentions from the palace. Most were either women or children. They pestered him with questions and, as he was well raised, he answered them as best and politely as he could.

'Are you going to fight with Achilles?' one woman said.

'No, I'm going to talk with him. I'm going to end the war.'

'Why do you have the sword and shield then?'

'Just a precaution.'

'Where do you come from?' a boy asked.

'Eriú. A land far north of here.'

'Hector!!'

'Are they all crazy where you come from?' another boy asked.

'Yes. We're all crazy.'

'Is it true about the beast? That you came with a monster?'

'Yes.'

'Is it going to end the war?'

'I am. Not the beast. Me.'

'You're very small. Are you sure you can take Achilles?' a girl said.

'Thanks, kid. Yes, I'm sure I can take him.'

'Why aren't you wearing armour?'

'Are you a barbarian?'

'Is it true that you run naked into battle?'

'Hector!!'

The questions became relentless and the crowd grew and grew until it was like a cloud of flies following him. And, all the time, Achilles called for Hector, his voice getting louder and louder as the Hound neared the gate. Finally, he was forced to give up his manners and good rearing, as it all became too much for him. He halted and roared, at the top of his voice, 'shut up!!!' The cloud dissipated almost instantly as the women and children fled in terror. He regretted it almost before it came out of him and, even though they had gone from him, he went on, apologetically, 'you're not making this easy for me. I have to get into a certain mindset if I am to meet this man. I need to stay concentrated and focused.' But he was talking to no one. So, he continued on his way to the main gate. Alone. Unhampered. And in silence. Complete silence.

For Achilles had stopped his roaring.

To get to the gate, he had to pass through hundreds of battle weary soldiers, all silenced by the great roar they had just heard from inside the city. Some were wounded and were being attended to. Some just sat there, exhausted. Others stood around in clusters. But all eyes were on him as he made his way through. There was fear and uncertainty in those eyes. But also hope. Who was this man from the North come to fight the enemy? Had Achilles at last met his match? But this hope evaporated when they got a closer look at the Hound. How could this small man with no armour seriously contend with Achilles? By the look of him he was not far out of boyhood. He might make a lot of noise but how could he realistically pose a threat to the great Achilles? So, many of the soldiers shook their heads and turned away from Cú Chulainn as he walked by.

He reached the gate. 'Open up!!' he roared.

The soldiers nearby sneered at him. 'He makes a big noise for such a small fellow,' one of them remarked. 'All bark and no bite, I'll bet,' said another.

Cú Chulainn ignored them but his pride did sting. It was an effort to keep his mind focused on what he had set out to do: end the war peacefully. The gates opened just a few feet to allow him to pass through.

Outside, he found Achilles waiting. He walked the hundred meters or so that separated them until he stood before him. Even taking his armour into account, Achilles was a big man. The biggest Cú Chulainn had ever faced. And, when he looked into his eyes, he found that the reports were true: Achilles was a madman. He remembered the premonition he had had upon entering the mind warp. 'My time,' Achilles had said. We'll have to see about that, he thought to himself.

'Are you the fellow who's making all the noise?' Achilles said.

Cú Chulainn nodded.

'So loud for such a slip of a thing! What are you doing here? Where's Hector?'

'I come in place of Hector. I come to sue for peace.'

'Peace? You'll have to ask the fool Agamemnon about that. He commands the Achaean army.'

'But they follow you.'

'I am in no mood for peace. Talk to me after I slay Hector. Where is he?' Achilles demanded.

'Don't you want to end this miserable war? You've been here nine years and what have you to show for it? Nothing but corpses.'

'I am no commander and no man commands me. I'm here to avenge the death of my friend, Patroclus. I don't care about the war.'

'But you have the power to end it.'

'Hector!!' Achilles bellowed once more.

'Please stop doing that,' the Hound said.

'Make me.'

'I know about you. Your fate is to die young in battle. Here in Troy. I have a similar fate. We have a lot in common.'

Achilles looked Cú Chulainn in the eye again but this time there was a ghost of reason there.

'Don't you see, we don't have to die? There is freedom within fate,' the Hound said.

'People will know my name and my deeds for thousands of years,' Achilles boasted.

'Same here, Achilles. Same here. But ask yourself, is it really worth it? You only get one life. Why throw it away so recklessly?'

'I've thought about my fate a great deal. But thinking about it is vain. I am destined to die here and there is nothing I can do about it. What is your name?'

'Cú Chulainn.'

'Where do you hail from?'

'A land far north of here. Named Eriú.'

'I'm sorry but you've come all this way for nothing. Go back into the city and I will wait here for Hector. You don't want to fight me.'

'I don't want to but I will if I have to,' the Hound said.

Achilles laughed and sneered and shook his head but he said nothing.

'Don't underestimate me, Achilles. A lot of men make that mistake. And they pay for it.'

'No man has ever bested me in combat. What makes you think you will do any different, whippersnapper!'

'Because I know you,' the Hound said and smiled.

'But we've never even met before.'

'Yes but I know you. Let's just say your fame has travelled far.'

'Then you should know that I am invincible.'

'Almost invincible.'

'Enough chit chat. If you want to try me, take your best shot,' Achilles said.

'You throw first,' Cú Chulainn said.

So, Achilles readied a spear and aimed. He let fly with tremendous force. Cú Chulainn dropped his sword and stood in the spear's trajectory. At the last millisecond, he turned his upper body and caught it mid-air.

'Nicely done,' Achilles said.

Cú Chulainn readied the spear and fired it back at Achilles. While it was still in the air, he picked up his sword and ran toward the other man with such speed that Achilles faced both spear and sword in the same millisecond.

Like Cú Chulainn had done, Achilles stayed where he was and at the last moment, he swatted away both the spear and sword of the Hound with his own blade.

'You have speed. For such a big man,' Cú Chulainn said as he walked back around to face Achilles again.

'Let's dance, Cú Chulainn. Seeing as you admire me so much.'

'I thought you'd never ask,' Cú Chulainn said and again ran at Achilles with sword readied. And Achilles ran at the Hound, until they met with a great clash. They fenced for a while. Achilles had great power and skill but Cú Chulainn used his size and lack of armour to his advantage, ducking and diving and bobbing and feigning and managing to nick Achilles several times. But never inflicting a serious wound.

'You dance well,' Achilles said, after they had disengaged. He was breathing heavily and his limbs shone with sweat from his exertions. But Cú Chulainn was still fresh, having no armour to weigh him down.

'Let's even things out a bit,' Achilles said and untied his breastplate, letting it fall to the ground.

At the sight of his opponent's great, powerful limbs and torso, the Hound felt a small pang of fear. For a second, he was tempted to use the Warp Spasm but he resisted, as it would be unfair. The men circled each other, warily. Respectfully.

When Cú Chulainn had said he knew Achilles, he wasn't lying. He knew that the man was invulnerable at all points of his body except for one small place: his right heel. He knew the story behind this. When Achilles was a baby, his mother, Thetis, had dipped him in the river Styx to make him invulnerable. And he was made so, all of him, except the heel by which his mother had held him. Cú Chulainn knew that if he could pierce this one small vulnerable place, he could maim Achilles and put him out of action for the remainder of the war. Without Achilles, the Achaeans would lose heart and give up. Go back to their ships and go home. At least, that was what he hoped would happen. So, he knew what he had to do. He had to get Achilles on his back so he could get to his right heel.

And this is how he did it.

Cú Chulainn's great advantage over Achilles was his speed. He was so much faster than the other man. If he was going to topple Achilles, he would need to play to this strength. So he did. Remembering what Hector had said to him about the shield following the sword, he sent his blade spinning toward Achilles like a throwing knife. Then, before Achilles could swat it away with his shield, Cú Chulainn ran at him again. Achilles dealt with the sword easily enough but had not the time to deal with the Hound who came after it, his shield readied for impact. Down went Achilles like a felled oak.

Cú Chulainn picked up his sword and, grabbing Achilles by his right foot, stood over him and said, 'I don't want to harm you, man. But I will if you don't concede and agree to go home.'

'Never.'

'This will maim you for life. Swallow your pride and let's end this war, peacefully. Nobody has to get hurt.'

'I don't command anyone. And nobody commands me.'

'Don't make me do this, Achilles.'

'What kind of a warrior are you?'

'It's not worth it. Concede, will you?'

'Never.'

Cú Chulainn sighed and shook his head. Then in one swift movement he sliced Achilles' heel. Blood spewed out of the wound, down Achilles leg, painting it red. The Achaean champion grimaced and groaned in complaint, his eyes wide. For it was the first real injury he had ever sustained in his life. The Hound let his foot go and looked down on him. He had just bested the greatest warrior who ever lived but he felt no pride or satisfaction, only pity and guilt. They stayed that way for a while, a grim tableaux from a grim tale of madness and wasted youth.

Then, the Hound heard something whistling in the air behind him. Before he could turn around he felt an explosion of pain in the centre of his back as something pierced it. He fell to his knees in agony.

'The coward!' Achilles cried, looking beyond the Hound toward the walls of Troy.

Cú Chulainn managed to turn around. He saw a lone bowman on the wall, standing with his weapon raised, as if in triumph.

He managed to say one word, with an excruciating gasp of pain, before he went under.

'Paris.'

IV

Journey to Cruachan

How did Laeg and Cathbad find out about Cú Chulainn's death and why did they journey to Cruachan?

It is soon told.

It was hard to believe that Cú Chulainn was dead. But what was even harder to believe were the rumours that he had died in his sleep. Everyone knew that the mad druid, Cathbad, was somehow involved but they were afraid to confront him about it. But even had they not been so, the druid could not be reached as he had shut himself up in his house and refused all visitors since the Hound had passed.

Yes, it was hard to believe that the Hound was dead. In fact, most people refused to believe it. This disbelief manifested itself in different ways: the fear of confronting Cathbad, the air of forced normality that pervaded the town, but the clearest manifestation was in the way the body had been treated. Instead of burning it, which was the way with all warriors of the Red Branch, Cú Chulainn's body had been placed inside a barrow, over which a mound had been raised. It was as if the people were waiting for him to rise and walk again through the muddy streets of Emain Macha. But Laeg knew differently. And so did Cathbad. They had been there when the life had been expelled out of him, at his very last breath.

The Hound had wanted knowledge and it seemed like he had paid the ultimate price for it. Apparently, he had escaped his fate, only to succumb to a worse one. Laeg had no idea where Cú Chulainn had travelled to on his quest for knowledge but whatever he had seen surely it couldn't be worth this. To die so peacefully and quietly, like an old man. Yes, Laeg was troubled for his best friend. For his legacy and his name. For his immortality. But mostly he just yearned to see him again. For Cú Chulainn was as a brother to him.

Inevitably, the young man turned to mead. He would go to the little river that ran past Emain Macha, where he and the Hound had met up most evenings to drink and talk. He drank deeply and the memories set his mind adrift. Memories of battle feats and fame, of chariot prowess and glory. Memories of wild oats sown, heroic gallivanting. Memories of their wedding days. Blissful days. Best days. But mostly he remembered the laughter and the sharing of secrets and songs as they sat here, drinking. Whiling away the hours. Feeling like it would never end.

But end it did, and Laeg was totally unprepared for it. All he could do was weep and sigh and groan, keeping his grief all to himself. He stopped washing and changing his clothes. He stopped eating. He shunned the company of all others except his wife. At times children who played by the river saw him, sitting at the bank, his shoulders shaking as he wept. What an awesome thing it was to see such a great warrior crying! But they knew that it was for Cú Chulainn. The Hound must have been a great warrior indeed to make this man grieve so terribly.

Of course, Laeg had made the circumstances of his friend's death known to his wife and parents, as well as King Conchobar. Yes, the rumours were true: he had died in his sleep. Or, at least, it was a kind of sleep. But beyond this, they were as much in the dark as the rest of the people. Just what had Cú Chulainn seen, what knowledge had he accessed, to exact such a terrible price? The question vexed Laeg greatly, and he felt like there would be no end to his mourning until it was answered.

'If you really want to know, go to Cathbad. Only he has the means of finding out.'

It was early in the afternoon and he was suffering from the after-effects of too much mead. His wife, Aisling, was in an unusually tolerant mood. She was talking to him. She even had a fry going for him. Pork and bacon sizzled on a hot plate while blue-grey smoke drifted and curled about the place, escaping through the thatching high above.

'Cathbad won't see anyone. He won't come out of his house,' he said to her.

'Surely, he'll see you. Weren't you with him when the Hound died?'

'I don't think he will. I don't think he wants to be reminded of it.'

Aisling sighed and said, 'You men can't bear much reality.'

'That's true, I suppose. I wonder what he is doing to help him cope. Probably taking lots of glamberries. I'd be afraid to call him out if he was off his head on those things.'

'Then you must accept not knowing.'

'No. I can't. I have to know what happened. Emain Macha has to know what happened. Don't you want to know how he died?'

'I know he died in his sleep. Maybe that's enough. Some would say that it is the best death.'

'Not for a warrior. A warrior deserves to die in battle, and Cú Chulainn was the greatest of us. He deserved a noble death.'

Aisling sighed again and said, 'sometimes things don't work out according to plan. Life is messy that way. You just have to live with it.'

'I refuse to. Not this time. I want to know how he really died.'

'Well then, go to Cathbad and find out what you want to know.'

'Ok, I will. I'll go there this afternoon.'

'It's already afternoon.'

'Ok, in the evening. When my head clears up,' he said, remembering his hangover. 'I don't know if I'll be able for that fry,' he said tentatively.

'You'd better be. I'm not throwing this out. You need to start eating again, Laeg. You've starved yourself quite enough.'

'Ok. Ok.'

'So, when are you going to stop all this drinking and hamming it up?'

'Hamming it up? What do you mean, hamming it up? You think what I feel isn't real?'

'I know you ache for him. I know that's real. But the drinking. Everything you do while you are drunk just isn't real. I'm sorry, but it isn't. I just want to know when you were planning on giving it up.'

'If you could feel how heavy my heart is when I think of him, you'd understand why I drink.'

'Maybe. But you can't keep drinking the way you are. Not unless you want to die too.'

'Maybe I do,' Laeg said with a sniff.

'And is that a good way for a warrior to die? Is that what you owe yourself? To drink yourself to death?'

'Good point, woman.'

'Don't *woman* me. Just tell me when you plan on giving it up.'

'Ok, Ok. I'll go to the druid this evening. If I can find out what happened to the Hound, I'll stop the drinking.'

'And if you can't find out?'

'Don't push me, Aisling. That's as far as I'll go, for now.'

His wife muttered something under her breath but, from the contented look on her face, it was plain to see that she was pleased.

Laeg arrived at Cathbad's house to find the entrance blocked off by a wooden door. The door was unhinged and so it had to be removed instead of opened to give way. Laeg called the druid a couple of times before he freed the door and stepped outside. He was in his usual scruffy and wild eyed state so it was hard to tell how the death of Cú Chulainn was affecting him. The two men stood there looking at each other in silence.

'Well?' Laeg said.

'Well what?'

'Aren't you at least going to invite me in?'

'No. The place is a mess. Talk out here. What do you want?' Cathbad said.

Laeg sighed and said, 'you know why I'm here, druid.'

'I can do many things Laeg Mac Riangabra but mind reading is not one of them,' the druid snapped.

'Don't be tetchy with me, old man.'

'What do you want?'

'I want to know how the Hound died.'

'The Hound died in his sleep. You were there weren't you?'

'He wasn't asleep, he was unconscious!'

'Yes. Yes.'

'Is that all you can say? *Yes, yes?*'

'What do you want me to say?'

'I want to know what happened to Cú Chulainn to take away his life. People don't just die like that. Not unless they are very old.'

'Cú Chulainn drank the milk of knowledge. Maybe he wanted to know what death is like.'

'Are you saying what I think you're saying?'

'I'm not saying anything, except who knows? We'll never know!'

'Are you not a druid?'

Cathbad sighed and said, 'yes.'

'You can contact the spirit world. Find out what happened.'

'Contacting the dead is a dangerous business, Laeg.'

'You are a druid. You know what to do.'

'If you get it wrong there is no telling what you might unleash,' Cathbad insisted.

'Don't lie to me, druid. Everyone knows you've been neglecting your duties ever since the Hound died. You just can't face up to it. Admit it.'

'Face up to what?' Cathbad said crossly.

'The truth.'

'Go home, Laeg. Leave me alone.'

'No, I won't. Not until you give me a good reason why you shouldn't do your duty and find out what happened.'

'I don't perform duties. I do what I like,' the druid said, half-heartedly.

'Ok, then do the right thing. By all of us who loved Cú Chulainn.'

'You think I didn't love him, too?'

'If you did then prove it! Contact the Otherworld.'

'I can't. I can't do it.'

'So, you didn't love him.'

'Don't say that, Laeg.'

'What else can I say? If you did love him you would do this.'

'Don't talk to me about love, boy!' the druid cried.

'Then what is it? Why won't you perform this task?'

'I told you, it's too dangerous.'

'I don't believe you. And you know what? I'm going to stay here until I get an honest answer out of you,' Laeg said.

'Ok, ok,' Cathbad said and let out a long, nervous sigh. 'Ok, boy. I'll tell you why. I can't do it because I feel so bloody guilty. I was the one who brought you to the Heifer. I explained the secret of her udder. Whatever happened to him, it was my fault. You're right. I just can't face up to it.'

'And I was the one whose idea it was to look for the Heifer in the first place. And I encouraged him to drink from her teat. You think I haven't been feeling guilty too? I know exactly how you feel, Cathbad. But we owe it to Cú

Chulainn to find out how he died. We owe it to his legacy. He was the greatest warrior Ulster has ever seen. Do you think he deserves the ignobility of being remembered as one who died in his sleep?'

'No,' the druid said and shook his head sadly.

'No. We owe it to him to find out the truth of his death. He was the Hound. The Warped One. The greatest warrior of our age. But more than this, Cathbad. More than this. He was our friend.'

'Aye. Aye. He was all those things,' the druid said, and Laeg could see his eyes were welling up. 'But he was more still. To me, that is. He was my blood.'

There was a shocked silence before Laeg said, 'your blood?'

'Yes! My blood!' Cathbad cried.

'How so your blood?'

'He was my grandson, Laeg.'

'Your grandson? Are you sure?'

'Of course I'm sure!' the druid snapped.

'Nobody ever told me,' Laeg said.

'That's because Cú Chulainn wanted it kept quiet. He was embarrassed by me.'

'I don't know what to say. I'm sorry, Cathbad.'

'It's ok. I understand why. I mean, wouldn't you be?'

There was another silence as Laeg searched for what to say. But words escaped him.

'So, now you might begin to understand the burden I bear. The guilt. My own grandson and I sent him to the Otherworld.'

'Now, wait a minute Cathbad. From what I remember, Cú Chulainn drank the milk of knowledge out of his own volition. We didn't force him. Nobody did.'

'Yes, but I drank it myself. Recklessly. I should have set a better example.'

'No, Cathbad. Cú Chulainn was a big lad. Big enough not to be influenced so easily.'

'No, Laeg. I was his grandfather. I should have been looking out for him,' the druid said.

'And I was his best friend. But you can't keep thinking like that. You'll drive yourself crazy. He's gone. There is nothing we can do about it. But what we can do is restore his legacy. We can find out the truth. Don't we owe it to him? To everyone?'

Cathbad looked at the young man, his eyes wet and fragile. He looked at him for what seemed like a long time before he said, 'Aye. We can do that, Laeg. We can do that. Give me a moment.'

The druid went back into his house. After a minute or so he emerged again with a bag slung over one shoulder and a water skin slung over the other, so that their straps crossed over his chest. 'Let's do this thing,' he said and the two men headed in the direction of the great temple at the top of the fort.

Once they were at the entrance to the temple, Laeg stopped and said, 'I'm not going in there.'

'Why not?'

'I'm afraid to. Isn't it forbidden for commoners to enter the temple? Besides, it's so dark!'

'Don't worry, Laeg. No harm will come to you.'

'Yes, but I feel like I'll be trespassing.'

'Don't you want to hear what Cú Chulainn has to say?'

'Yes. Of course,' Laeg said.

'Then come on. I'm not doing this without you.'

So, they entered the temple. Inside, there was a strong spicy scent in the air, but behind it was the unmistakeable odour of animal flesh. Laeg shuddered to think of all the bulls and heifers that must have been sacrificed here.

'Let me just light the fire,' the druid said. Laeg saw sparks as Cathbad made to strike up a flame. When he had done so, he coaxed it and fed it with tinder before dropping it onto the remains of the previous fire. He added some timber and, once he was satisfied with it, he looked at Laeg, and said, 'this way.' They moved away from the fire, deeper into the interior of the temple, until they stood before a large, square block of stone with the effigy of a human head hewn out of the top of it. The head's mouth was wide open and appeared to be stained, inside and outside, either black or red – it was hard to make out in the firelight. Like everyone in Emain Macha, Laeg was well aware of the power associated with the human head as an object of magic and divination. So, he remained silent as the druid went about his business. First, he took out a silver chalice from his bag and placed it beside the effigy. Then, opening the waterskin, he poured the contents into the chalice until it was nearly full. Next, he produced from his bag a small knife. He promptly sliced his left thumb and let the blood fall into the chalice. 'For gods, animal blood. For mortals, human blood,' he said to Laeg by way of explanation. When he was satisfied that enough blood had been let into the chalice, he picked it up and holding it over the effigy's mouth, made the following incantation: 'blood to mouth. Blood to blood. Blood to spirit. Blood to earth.' Then he poured the contents into the stained mouth, until the chalice was empty. The stone mouth held the liquid but not for long, as it drained away into the darkness at its throat.

'Where does that go to?' Laeg said.

'The earth.'

'How deep?'

'Nobody knows. Deep enough,' the druid said. 'Cú Chulainn!' he then cried softly. 'Hound! Are you there? I want to talk to you.' This was met with silence. 'I want to speak to the Warped One. Are you there?' Cathbad said. There was another silence. 'Cú Chulainn, it's Cathbad and Laeg. We want to talk to you.'

'Cathbad? Laeg?' a voice answered. It was distant and somewhat distressed but undeniably the Hound's.

'Yes! It's us! Where are you?' the druid said.

'Where do you think I am! I'm in the Otherworld! What do you want?'

'We want to know what happened. How you died,' the druid said.

There was a long silence and Cathbad worried that the connection had been lost, but eventually the Hound answered. 'Long story short. I travelled to Ancient Troy. To see Helen. I got into a fight with Achilles and, just after I had bested him, I got an arrow in the back from the bow of Paris, for my troubles. That's what killed me,' the Hound said. His voice was uneven, as if carried to them by a ragged wind.

'I knew it! A warrior's death!' Laeg cried.

'But how did it kill you? If you travelled there mentally? That's what I want to know,' Cathbad said.

'I don't know. I guess the body can't live without the mind.'

'Possibly,' the druid said.

'Where are you in the Otherworld?' Laeg said.

'I'm with Her.'

'Her?'

'The Queen. I'm her prisoner. Ah, Cathbad! Laeg! You have to get me out of here! I don't belong in this world! Not yet!'

'What would you have us do?' the druid said, eagerly.

'Come to the Otherworld and get me!'

'How?' Laeg said. 'Tell us how.'

'I don't know. There must be a way. An entrance. Find it,' Cú Chulainn said.

There was a silence. Laeg looked at the old druid for an answer. He appeared abstracted.

'You have to get me out of here!' Cú Chulainn cried. 'I shouldn't be here. It's not my time...' The voice died out like a flame touched by a zephyr.

'Cú Chulainn? Are you there?' Laeg cried.

'He's gone.'

'So fast?'

'Yes. That's all you get. A half a minute.'

'Well?'

'Well what?"

'Is there a way to the Otherworld? We have to go there and rescue Cú Chulainn.'

'Yes, there is a way. But I don't know how we can get him back. He is in the spirit world now. His body lies dead in that barrow.'

'We can cross that bridge when we come to it. Where is it?'

'It's in Cruachan. In Connacht.'

'Cruachan? You mean Medb's country?'

'Medb's country. Yes.'

'Do you think she'll let us use it?'

'I don't know. Technically, we are still at war. And Cú Chulainn almost wiped out her army. If she finds out why we want to go to the Otherworld she might deny us. No, I think the best thing to do would be to make our way there quietly and slip into the entrance without her knowing. We'll disguise ourselves as vagabonds.'

'Vagabonds?'

'Yes. So no one will give us a second glance. We'll be like ghosts,' the druid said.

'When do we leave?'

'Tomorrow. Why wait?'

'Ok. What about my Aisling? Should I tell her?'

'Yes but no one else. We must keep this business as quiet as possible. That will give us the best chance of success.'

'Have you ever been there before? The Otherworld, I mean.'

'No,' Cathbad said.

'But you know what you are doing, right?'

'Not really.'

'I appreciate your honesty, druid. But your words are not exactly inspiring.'

Ignoring this, Cathbad said, 'go to your wife and say goodbye to her. Get dressed in the foulest rags you can find. Meet me at my house at dawn.'

Laeg did as he was told. He couldn't find anything suitable for a vagabond to wear so he went out in search of the local tramp, MacSuirtain. When he found him he made an offer of an exchange of his attire for the tramp's 'rags'. The tramp refused, saying it was an insult to his dignity but he said he might consider giving up his clothes for the handsome torc that Laeg wore around his neck. Laeg cursed him but agreed. So, the tramp stepped out of the rags he wore and accepted the torc. He put it on and then ran away, naked and laughing, into the twilight. Laeg shook his head in dismay and disgust, picking up the bundle of rags.

He met Cathbad outside his house as dawn took to her throne in the east. It was chilly, especially in the new clothes he had acquired. He rubbed his hands vigorously and ran on the spot in an effort to ward off the cold. When Cathbad emerged, he looked Laeg up and down before nodding in approval. But the druid appeared to be dressed in his usual attire: a dirty, stained white robe.

'That's not fair! You said we were to dress as vagabonds! Both of us!' Laeg cried.

'I am dressed as a vagabond. To a foreigner's eye. You're just used to seeing me wear this.'

'But I'm freezing!'

'You'll get used to it.'

'But—'

'Now stop your complaining and let's be on our way.'

It took them about a week's walking to get to Cruachan. They stayed off the main pathways, keeping to the heavy forest that covered most of the island at that time. Cathbad had never been to the Otherworld but he had been to Cruachan on many occasions, so he knew how to get there. When asked, he explained how he had visited the place often, before the war over the Brown Bull, to exchange knowledge and lore with Medb's druid, Feargus.

'Ah, those were Halcyon days, my friend,' Cathbad reminisced. 'Two great centres of Gaelic civilisation. Prospering and at peace. There is so much two peoples can learn from each other when they are not at war. The exchange of knowledge and technology is always better than the exchange of death and corpses.'

'Will there ever be a permanent peace, Cathbad?' Laeg asked.

'Maybe. There may come a time when we are a shining example to the rest to the world. But it won't be in my lifetime. That's for sure.'

Laeg sighed and said, 'how can people go to war over a dumb animal like a bull? I mean, when you think about it, it's crazy.'

'Yes, it is. But all war is madness. It goes against the grain of reason, imagination, wisdom and all that is good in human nature. It's why I'm a pacifist.

'What is a pacifist?'

'We believe that no war is justifiable. It's a good way to think. You should try it.'

'Hmmm. Maybe I will.'

'But keep it quiet, Laeg, won't you? It's a bit radical and I'm unpopular enough as it is.'

'Don't worry. Your secret's safe with me.'

'But you've changed your tune. What about all your talk about dying a heroic death in battle?' the druid said.

'Yes, it's part of the warrior's code. But only in times of war. I want peace and prosperity as much as you do.'

'But that code helps to perpetuate a state of war. Like I said, the exchange of corpses is the business of warfare.'

'I don't have the wits to argue with you, Cathbad.'

'It's ok. To contradict one's self is natural. Especially in a young man.'

So, quietly and steadily, they made their way through the trees, resting in the mellow evenings and setting out again in the brisk mornings. Luckily, the weather was on their side. Had it rained, it would have made life very uncomfortable for the travellers, but it hadn't. The days were crisp and overcast. The air was pungently bittersweet. The essence of autumn.

Cathbad led the way, striking the ground with his staff after every few steps he made. He showed an energy that surprised Laeg. He had never seen the old druid so mobile and determined in his gait. And it seemed to increase as they got closer to Medb's country. As if he were being drawn to Cruachan and the entrance to the Otherworld. As they rarely talked when travelling, Laeg waited until they were settled down for the evening to ask the druid about this.

Cathbad stared moodily into the small fire they had made. Every evening, the same fire, almost as if it travelled with them from Emain Macha. A little piece of home. The druid picked the twigs off a small branch he was holding and tossed them into the flames, slowly, one by one.

'I won't lie to you Laeg. Greatly does my heart desire this. To see the Otherworld. At last.'

'But you said you've been to Cruachan before. Many times. Why didn't you visit it on those occasions?' Laeg said.

'Because I was afraid.'

'And you're not now?'

'Let me tell you something about life, boy. The older you get, the more you fear this world but the less you fear the afterlife.'

'I'm not afraid.'

'That's because you think you are immortal. Sub-consciously, I mean. But you will fear it. In time.'

'It makes no difference to me. I just want to get Cú Chulainn back,' Laeg said.

'It will be difficult. We have to get him back body and soul and, I must admit, this perplexes me.'

'Has anyone ever done it before? Come back from the dead, I mean?' Laeg asked.

'Not that I know of.'

'Well, if anyone can do it, Cú Chulainn can. Right?'

'Maybe.'

'Will he be changed? When he comes back?'

'O yes. Inevitably. Irrevocably. I think it's fair to say that we will never see the old Cú Chulainn again. But don't fret about it. Change happens to us all. If it doesn't happen at least once, you've wasted your life.'

They had many conversations like this, the old druid dispensing wisdom and Laeg taking it all in but not without questions here and there. He was seeing another side to Cathbad. A mellow and generous side that the charioteer had only glimpsed before. For the first time, he could imagine the druid as a grandfather. Again, this change in personality seemed to grow as they got nearer to Cruachan. Laeg reasoned that it was because he was getting closer to his grandson, Cú Chulainn. He had said that the Hound was ashamed of him. Judging by this new turn in his character, Cú Chulainn would have to change his mind. If they both survived the Otherworld, that is.

Cathbad's hopes of slipping into the entrance to the Otherworld unnoticed were ended when they were arrested by a couple of Medb's soldiers, just outside the town of Rathcruachan. They were talking by the fire when the men approached. After the druid complained that they were just a couple of travellers, one of the warriors said, 'we know who you are. You are Cathbad, the druid of Emain Macha. You must come with us. Queen Medb wishes to see you.'

The druid grumbled and told Laeg to get their things together.

'This wouldn't have happened if we were both dressed as vagabonds,' Laeg whispered sharply. Cathbad grumbled some more, unleashing a few curses under his breath as well.

The attitude of the soldiers showed that they were in no immediate danger. It was clear that they feared and respected him.

Medb's men brought them through the streets of Rathcruachan, one leading and one bringing up the rear. It was dark, so they couldn't see much, but it smelled and sounded just like Emain Macha at night.

They came to Medb's great stone roundhouse. One of the soldiers indicated that they should go in. When they did so, they were not followed by either of the men, which surprised Laeg.

Inside, at the centre of the floor of the house, was a powerful fire. Its flames shed a dancing light on the room, giving tantalising glimpses of lavish tapestries that adorned the stone walls. Laeg's eye was drawn to them. He couldn't help it, they were so beautiful and compelling.

'Impressed?' a female voice said. 'Come closer so's I can get a better look at you.' She spoke in a slow but melodious accent.

Laeg tore his eyes away from the tapestries and walked around the fire to where Cathbad stood before the Queen of Cruachan.

She sat on a burnished wooden throne which was draped in furs and pelts. A very handsome and voluptuous woman in a blue robe that revealed a milk-white shoulder and a generous amount of cleavage but which was girdled by a great leather belt above her broad hips. She had an easy smile. In fact everything about her seemed easy. Her posture, her attitude, her hooded eyes. But she also emanated great power.

She was surrounded by animals. A fox lay across her shoulder, snuggling up to her neck. A cat rested in her lap, composed but alert to the two strangers. At her feet were two hounds – a Great Dane which lay with its snout resting on the ground, sleeping quietly and an Irish Wolfhound which sat nearby, panting, its eyes reflecting the fire.

There was also a strange, complex aroma in the air. It was sweet and flowery and feminine but was infused with other smells that Laeg couldn't put a name to. But whatever it was made up of, it was potent.

Overwhelmed by the sight of the Queen and the strange scent that ruled the air, the young man's legs turned to jelly and he fell down on his knees.

Medb laughed and said, 'you don't have to kneel to me, my good man. I am a queen but I am not your queen.'

'I can't help it,' Laeg said and his voice sounded thick and heavy and distant to his ears.

Medb laughed some more and he heard Cathbad say, 'don't worry, son. It happens to us all.'

'Not all, evidently,' Medb said.

'I became immune to your, eh, charms a long time ago, Queen Medb.'

'You don't find me beautiful anymore?'

'More than ever. But my legs have become old and stubborn, Queen.'

'A good answer. Strange but…you always were a strange sort, weren't you?'

'I'm a druid. It goes with the territory,' Cathbad said and beamed at the monarch. 'Can I ask how you learned of our approach?'

'You know I have my spies, Cathbad.'

'Of the winged variety?'

'Yes.'

'Ah, I should have known.'

'You will tell me why you have come here, druid. But first tell me who is this fine young fellow who accompanies you.'

'His name is Laeg. He is Cú Chulainn's charioteer and best friend.'

'Ah, I thought this had something to do with the Hound.'

'You've learned of his passing?' Cathbad said.

'Yes, of course. A great loss. He was my enemy but he was a worthy one.'

'Thank you, Queen.'

'Convey my respects to his family and King Conchobar.'

'Again, thank you, Queen. You are most gracious. But that might not be necessary. We've come to ask your permission to use the passage to the Otherworld. We are going to try to bring Cú Chulainn back.'

'Are you serious?'

'Yes.'

'A bold venture, druid. So, you planned on sneaking in without my knowing? Is that it?'

'Yes, Queen.'

'And why wouldn't I allow you to use the entrance?'

'Because Cú Chulainn almost wiped out your entire army. You would have taken the Brown Bull if it wasn't for him. He was your sworn enemy.'

'But a worthy one, as I have said.'

'You will let us use the passage?'

Medb looked down and stroked the cat in her lap and seemed distracted for a few moments. Then she looked up at the druid again and said, 'yes, I will allow it. Though it goes against my instinct and reason. He was a great warrior and he deserves a better death. Hopefully it will be at the hands of one of my men. If you get him back that is. As far as I know, no one has ever done it. It would be quite a feat.'

'There is something else, Queen. Something that you might not have heard of. The Donn Cuailgne has returned to Emain Macha.'

'The Brown Bull is back? I thought him dead.'

'So did I but it seems he has defied us. But there is more. A great heifer has turned up as well. I believe it is a good sign. A sign of peace and prosperity. The old bull is finally going to settle down and take a wife, as it were.'

'You mean peace between our peoples? Or just for yours?'

'Peace for all of us on this island.'

Medb seemed to consider this before saying, 'tell Conchobar I've no more designs on the Brown Bull. I lost enough of my men trying to claim him.'

'I will.'

'And take this,' the Queen said, reaching into her cleavage to produce a small vial that was hung around her neck by a silver lace. She removed it over her golden head and handed it to the druid. 'It's an aphrodisiac. For the bull. Give him a couple of snorts of this and he'll be aroused.'

'Another sign of peace! You give us access to the Otherworld and you give us one of your most secret potions. How can we repay you?' the druid said.

'Don't rush things, druid. Cú Chulainn's actions caused much bitterness in the people of Rathcruachan. Myself included. If there is to be peace it will take time. But accept my gifts as a gesture of good will.'

Cathbad bowed and said, 'and it will not go unanswered.'

'Now, you wish to use Oweynagat.'

'I'm sorry, Queen?'

'Oweynagat. The Cave of the Cats. The entrance to the Otherworld?'

'Ah, yes. It's been a while since I was last here.'

'You're a druid. You're supposed to remember these things. You've got a trained mind.'

'Yes but I'm getting old. No amount of training or exercise can prevent that. Deterioration is inevitable.'

'Don't depress me, old man.'

'I'll be out of your way as soon as you tell me where the cave is, Queen.'

'Find Feargus and he will take you there. You do remember Feargus, don't you?'

'Yes, of course. Where will I find him?'

'Ask one of the guards outside. Now, leave me and take this poor fellow with you.'

'Thank you, Queen. For everything,' Cathbad said. Then he put his arms around Laeg's trunk and whispered sharply, 'get up!' When the young man didn't respond, he whispered again, 'get up, fool!' He was eager to be out of there, afraid that Medb would change her mind. 'Laeg! Stand up!' The young man managed to get onto his feet. He took one more look at the Queen and she smiled at him, whilst stroking the fox on her shoulder, and then he turned around and let the druid guide him out of the house. But she wasn't finished with them.

'By the way!' she called.

Cathbad managed to turn himself and Laeg around to face the Queen.

'Say hello to my Other. If you see her.'

Cathbad didn't know who her Other was, but he thought better not to question her. He merely nodded his head and said, 'of course.'

Then he and Laeg turned around again and left the house of the Queen of Cruachan.

V

Journey to the Otherworld

How did Cathbad and Laeg reclaim the soul of Cú Chulainn?

It is soon told.

Feargus led them to a sacred grove where he and Cathbad could talk more freely. On the way, Laeg's strength returned gradually. By the time they had reached the place, he was fully recovered. Now, he stood in the darkness, enjoying the soft wind and the perfume of the trees, as Cathbad and Feargus conversed quietly nearby. Feargus was a bald and bearded man with a sunny disposition. He had large brown eyes that were soft and serene. He and Cathbad got on very well, which was surprising seeing as they were so different. Although they were too far away for Laeg to hear what they were saying, there was no argument in their voices, only a kind of tense and subdued exchange. They talked in this way for about twenty minutes before returning to Laeg.

'Feargus will bring us to the Cave of the Cats. But we must go blindfolded,' Cathbad said.

'I'm sorry, young Laeg, but the cave is one of the most carefully kept secrets in all of Ireland.'

'That's ok with me.'

'Good lad,' Feargus said and produced two silken scarves from his robe.

'They look fine! Where did you get those?' Cathbad said.

'A gift. From a Persian prince.'

'On one of your odysseys, I take it?'

'Yes. You know how I like to travel.'

The druid of Rathcruachan then gently tied the scarves around their heads and they were made temporarily blind.

'Laeg, put your hand on Cathbad's shoulder. Cathbad, you put your hand on mine. I'll lead.'

They did as they were told and then set off on the secret path to Oweynagat.

Nobody said a word. It seemed appropriate to remain silent given the significance and sacredness of the place they were travelling to: the only known entrance to the Otherworld in all the land. Laeg desired greatly to see the place. He had never had much of an imagination but as they approached the cave his mind filled with images of beauty and grandeur. The mighty works of the divine and the immortal. A city and people of such sublimity they could only be glimpsed by the human mind. And, overlooking it all, a great queen with flashing eyes, enthroned in shadows. These thoughts crowded his mind and he didn't know if it was the blindfold or the proximity to the cave that stimulated them. Yes, he longed to see the Otherworld. The sheer boldness of what they were doing excited him. Who knew what they would encounter? Nobody just walked into paradise and walked back out again. And as for stealing a soul? He had said to Cathbad that they would cross that bridge when they came to it. Well, now they were approaching that bridge and he still had no idea of how they were going to bring the Hound back. This scared him but it also elated him. Yes, they were in the dark, both literally and figuratively, but with the dark comes the promise of discovery and this set Laeg's blood to singing and his young mind to further reverie.

Before the entrance to Oweynagat, Feargus removed their blindfolds. It was at the end of a sudden, steep decline in the forest ground, like a stairway but without the steps. A large opening supported by a wooden lintel and jambs.

'I was expecting something more...'

'Impressive, Laeg?' Feargus said.

'Yes. Why do they call it the Cave of the Cats?'

'Well, according to legend, this cave was once guarded by three fierce leopards. They would attack anyone who dared enter.'

'What happened to them?'

'Nobody knows.'

'Feargus, do many people visit this place?'

'No. Just myself, these days.'

Laeg nodded and said no more.

Medb's druid shook their hands and made a swift departure. It seemed like he was in a hurry to escape the place. Once inside, they found that there were bones covering every inch of the ground. Centuries of bones. They stumbled on them in the darkness, like two inebriates. Cathbad put an arm around the younger man's shoulders.

'This is a nightmare,' Laeg said.

'It won't last.'

'Are all these bones from sacrifices?'

'Yes.'

'I'm really starting to regret this, Cathbad.'

'No turning back now. We've come this far.'

So, they continued to make their way over the bones. Laeg nearly fell a couple of times. The thought of falling on this skeletal carpet made him shudder.

'So, what did you make of Queen Medb?' Cathbad asked the young man, in an attempt to distract him.

'I don't remember much about the meeting to be honest with you.'

Cathbad laughed and said, 'it happens to most men who see her for the first time.'

'I felt completely…spent. She is an incredibly beautiful woman.'

'Yes. The most beautiful and powerful in all the land.'

'I guess she really likes animals too, huh?'

'Yes, indeed. I think she draws on their power. I believe it's why she coveted the Brown Bull.'

'I still can't believe she went to war over a bull.'

'She's a determined woman. She gets what she wants. But she did say she has no more designs on him. And she gave me a gift for Conchobar. An aphrodisiac for the Bull. It'll make him fall in love with the Heifer. Ah, Laeg, peace is in the air. I know it.'

'I hope so,' the young man said.

The bones became fewer and fewer. Soon, they found themselves walking on a level floor. The only thing they experienced was the sound of their breathing and their footfalls, and Cathbad's staff as it struck the ground. All their other senses were made inactive. It was an eerie sensation. Sometimes, they exchanged a few words in whispers, fearful that their voices would carry and alert someone or something. They hadn't forgotten that they were trespassers in this place.

After a while, Laeg began to feel the stirrings of claustrophobia and panic inside him. Although they weren't in a confined space, the darkness and emptiness that silenced his senses made it feel like they were entombed.

'I don't think I can take much more of this,' he whispered.

'Relax and keep walking.'

'It feels like we've been buried alive.'

'Don't say that!' the druid whispered sharply. 'Just think of Emain Macha. Think of having a midnight stroll through the wood.'

'I think we made a bad mistake coming here, druid.'

'Shhhhh. Let's pick up our pace. I'm sure something will happen eventually.'

All Laeg needed was the slightest distraction. The smallest sensation beyond the sound of their passing through the cave. Just to make him feel like he was alive again. And it came just in the nick of time.

'It's getting lighter,' Cathbad said after stopping.

Laeg stopped too. He looked around and found that the druid was right. It was getting lighter. And he could see the source of the luminescence. Tiny veins of silver ran along the surfaces of the walls on either side of them. Just bright enough to be seen. They had no pattern but at that moment they were as beautiful as the finest brooch ever made, to Laeg's eyes.

'Let's move on!' Cathbad said with renewed confidence.

As they made their way, the veins in the rock branched out and multiplied. Soon they resolved themselves into patterns. Spirals and curvilinear forms that became more luminescent as the travellers went deeper.

Laeg stopped to admire the beautiful handicraft of the immortals. For who else could have fashioned this wonder? So intricate and delicate and ingenious!

'No. You mustn't do that,' Cathbad said, pulling the blonde young man away from the wall.

'But it's so beautiful!' Laeg protested.

'And dangerous. If you get too involved in it, your soul will be trapped for aeons. And we don't have that much time.'

'How do you know?'

'I've heard many tales about the Otherworld and they all caution against this kind of thing. Beauty is dangerous in this place. Now, come on!'

They continued on through the tunnel but it became harder for Laeg to resist the draw of the beautiful handicraft of the walls. Here and there the patterns turned into concrete representations. Mostly heads. Human heads and animal heads. But birds as well, and otters and foxes and other native creatures of the land.

Cathbad dragged him away from the walls, sometimes knocking him on the head with his staff. This seemed to do the trick. But for how long?

Then, to the druid's relief, they heard distant music. Finally, something to focus on and to keep Laeg's mind off the perilous walls.

'Do you hear that?' the druid said.

'Yes. I hear music. Do you think someone knows we are here?'

'Possibly. Anyway, there is nothing we can do about it. Let's just keep walking.'

As the music got louder, Cathbad became more and more impressed by it. It was easily the most complex and sophisticated music he had ever heard. It came from a single instrument and it seemed to emulate the sound of a woman keening at a graveside.

They continued through the tunnel and all the time the walls became more luminescent. When at last they came to the source of the music, it was almost as bright as day. A man sat on a rock with a bag in his lap. There were sticks protruding from the bag and he manipulated them with his hands as he pressed the bag with his forearm, almost like a bellows. It seemed to take considerable strength and skill. He continued to play, intent on his instrument, as the strangers watched and listened.

Cathbad was no stranger to musical instruments. The people of Emain Macha boasted many musicians and they each had their speciality: the carnyx, the lyre, the horn. But none of them could compete with the power and precision of the music he was hearing now. It seemed to him to have a perfection of form and content. His mind glowed and his heart flooded with feeling. He looked at Laeg and saw that he, too, was affected by the music. His eyes were soft and transported. His face passive.

The man continued to play. There were turns and nuances in the music and he constantly shifted from a major to a minor key and back again, until it felt like he was playing, not just the instrument, but Cathbad's heart too. It was an intense feeling. Almost too intense. Just as he was beginning to feel like it was unbearable, a woman seemed to come out of nowhere to stand behind the musician. She put a hand on his shoulder and he stopped playing. For the first time he looked at his audience. He had strange, impenetrable eyes and he didn't smile.

'Welcome, travellers,' the woman said. She was tall and graceful, with white-golden hair and a crimson robe. Her eyes were soft but she too didn't smile.

'Thank you, lady,' Cathbad said.

'You've come this far. I expect you have some questions?'

'What is that instrument this gentleman plays?' the druid said.

'It's called the uilleann pipes. It's a few centuries ahead of your time. Did you like it?'

'I've never been moved so much by any music, lady.'

'Yes, they are the purest expression of the spirit of the Gael. That's why they are played here, at the threshold of the spirit world.'

'I see,' said Cathbad.

'You mean we've made it? To the Otherworld?' Laeg said.

'You are almost there,' the woman said and reached into the pockets of her crimson robe. She produced two silver-coated apples, one in each hand. Then she tossed them, one by one, to the travellers, who caught them.

Laeg looked at the strange fruit in his hand. It was so smooth and shiny! He raised it to his nose and sniffed it.

'It is not for eating, Laeg,' the woman said with a hint of a smile.

'Then what?' Cathbad said.

'They will allow you to pass through the Otherworld as mortals. Unhindered. Just think of them as passports.'

'Passports?' the druid said.

'Sorry. Way ahead of your time. The silver apples will give you access to the spirit world without having to die first.'

'Thank you, lady. We appreciate your help. You know of our mission?'

'Yes, of course. You've come to bring back Cú Chulainn from the dead.'

'Do you know how we can do it?' Laeg spoke up. 'Because we have no idea.'

'No, Laeg. You must find a way by yourselves. Bring Cú Chulainn back from the dead. For his soul yearns to return. This is your task and you must not fail,' the lady said and there was an undercurrent of emotion in her voice which frightened Laeg a little. He feared what might happen if she unleashed that emotion. Then, as if on cue, the piper started to play again. This seemed to signal an end to the conversation. The woman stood behind the master musician, with a hand on his shoulder and her head bowed a little.

Laeg looked at the druid with a questioning eye. Cathbad merely shrugged and indicated that he should follow him.

And so they passed on into the Otherworld.

The realm of the dead was beautiful to behold.

The sky was a deep, velvet blue which transitioned into dark purple. There was a strange crescent moon that looked like the tip of a woman's finger nail. There were no stars. Besides the alien moon, it was just a swathe of dark heaven, eternally veiled.

The people seemed to emanate their own light, moving through the metropolis like parades of ghost flames. They came in all shapes and sizes but most were young and lean and radiant of eye. To Laeg they were like creatures that had come out of the shadows. They weren't necessarily aesthetically perfect but they were perfect in their own way.

As with the music they had heard earlier, the two travellers had never witnessed such complex and sophisticated buildings. There really was not much difference in the technology and techniques used to create these edifices when compared to the world above, but they had a precision and grandeur that was wholly lacking in the mortal realm. Some had features that both men had never seen before: chimneys to let the smoke out and porticos with pillars of stone. But how well-crafted they were! The thatches were perfectly fashioned and looked as strong as iron and the stone work was impossibly smooth and precise. They also looked well planned. In fact the entire metropolis was a lesson in how to plan a city. No clusters of houses, no ad hoc buildings, everything just straight and level. And all paths and roads intersecting.

It was also clean. There was no muck on the thorough-fares, no sewage. Everything was hard and dry and spotless. There were vagabonds in the city but they looked happy and dignified. Like they were indispensable. And it smelled nice. A pleasing mixture of aromas: smoke and spice and cooked meat and other olfactory delights.

So, the city of the dead was bright and beautiful and, it turned out, completely oblivious to the presence of the two visitors.

'Why can't they see us?' Laeg said.

'It's the apples the lady gave us. Believe me, I'd be more worried if they *could* see us.'

'But how are we going to find the house of the Queen?'

'Let's just walk a while. Maybe something will turn up,' the druid said.

And so they entered the flow of the inhabitants of the Otherworld metropolis.

Laeg noticed that there were vibrant colours everywhere: in the clothes of the inhabitants, in the fruits on display at the stalls, in the thatching of the rooves. But it was all envel-oped in a numinous, silvery sheen, which gave the place a dream quality.

'It's so beautiful. I don't know how they managed to build it,' Laeg said.

'The dead have a lot of time on their hands.'

'One thing I don't understand, though. If these people are the dead, or spirits of the dead, why do they have things like food and warmth and shelter?'

'Because this is a reflection of our world,' Cathbad explained.

'But it is so different! It's so much finer!'

'The mirror lies, Laeg. The mirror tells us that we are better than what we are. It flatters us.'

They fell into a silence, all the time passing through the crowds of ghosts. Even the ghost voices sounded better than any mortal's. The general social hum sounded like some great, complex chord, lovely and never-ending. The hawkers sang their hearts out and there came to them, carried in waves, fragments of music accompanied by the finest vocals.

After a while, Laeg sighed.

'What is it, Laeg?' the druid asked.

The young man sighed again before saying, 'this place is starting to get to me. Everyone is so beautiful and radiant.'

Cathbad laughed and said, 'remember we shouldn't be here. We are trespassers.'

'I know. I just wish we could find the Queen's place and get the Hound,' Laeg said. Then he stopped, as something suddenly occurred to him. He slapped his forehead with the palm of his hand. The druid stopped too and turned around to face him.

'What is it, Laeg?'

'I just realised. How can we get Cú Chulainn back when he can't even hear or see us?'

'We'll work something out,' Cathbad said.

'But nobody can see us, Cathbad! You said it yourself. We are trespassers.'

'I reckon that crow can see us.'

'What crow?'

'Over there. On that wheelbarrow.'

Laeg looked about and spotted the bird, perched on one of the handles of the wooden vehicle.

'That's no crow, Cathbad. Its feathers are white.'

'Yes, it is. It's a white crow. It's been following us.'

'Are you sure?'

'Yes. I think it's a sign. That we should follow it.'

'But it's only a bird, Cathbad,' Laeg said.

'Do not dismiss the power and accuracy of bird lore, young man. There is so much you can read into their behaviour. They are often servants or messengers of the divine. This bird is unnatural, just like we are in this realm. So, it is a sign. We must follow it.'

'Ok, if you're sure,' Laeg said.

Cathbad sighed and said, 'do you have any better ideas?'

'No. Not at the moment.'

'Then we follow the bird,' the druid said and, as if on cue, the white crow flew off the wheelbarrow and disappeared behind some thatching.

So, they followed the bird. Always they would lose sight of it as it went over a building or a roof but they soon caught up with it again. Laeg started to believe that the druid might be right. There could be something in this.

It went on for the better part of half an hour, the bird giving no respite. Finally it seemed to arrive at a destination. A giant, grey complex building which we would know as a castle. It was situated in a field just outside the city walls, which the travellers walked through without meeting any resistance. The walls of the castle were covered in ivy, blue and purple to reflect the colours of the sky. The travellers were a little awestruck by the residence, it was so far ahead of their time. They were intimidated too. It was certainly no reflection of any buildings they knew from the world above. Cathbad had travelled much during his years and this was the first time he had seen a royal house that was not at the centre of the metropolis it ruled over.

But they were relieved at having found the Queen of the Otherworld's dwelling. For who else could live in such grandeur? The strange crescent moon seemed to hang just above it and the sky beyond it glowed as if in pleasure. Cathbad was reminded of the uillean pipes he had heard in the cave. They, too, were ahead of their time. Were they glimpsing some future golden age?

But instead of flying directly to the royal building, the crow went to the shoulder of a man who sat on a rock a few hundred yards away from the entrance. So, they walked toward this man. As they got closer, Cathbad could see that the man was holding a lyre but he had stopped playing it to listen to the bird on his shoulder.

It was Laeg who recognised him first. It was none other than Cú Chulainn! Even here in the realm of the radiant, the Hound stood out. He was that beautiful. But he also stood out because he was so sorrowful. It broke Laeg's heart to see him like this.

The Hound listened to the bird on his shoulder. Then, looking in the general direction of the travellers, he spoke thus: 'this bird tells me that you have come for me at last, Cathbad and Laeg. If this is true, I yearn to see you and talk to you again. You must go to the Queen and get her to release me. For I don't belong here. Not yet. I've been sitting here trying to learn how to play this thing but it's a waste of time. It's all a waste of time!' The Hound then shook his head and tears of sorrow and frustration traversed his cheeks. Laeg, seeing his friend suffering so, went over to embrace him. Three times he tried to put his arms around him and three times he failed. It was as if they were passing through smoke.

Cathbad walked over to Laeg and put a hand on his shoulder to comfort him for it was obvious that he was in great distress. 'Come. Let's see the Queen. Let's make the deal,' the druid said.

The outside of the building reflected no structure the two travellers had ever seen but inside, in the throne room, there were many things they recognised. Especially from Queen Medb's royal house. The fire was off to the side in a fireplace but everything else mirrored the great roundhouse of Rathcruachan: the tapestries that tantalised on the walls, the great wooden throne that was hung with animal furs and pelts and the Queen herself who sat surrounded by animals. Cathbad now understood what Medb had meant by her 'other'. This was her reflection in the spirit realm. The Queen of the Otherworld. Of course, there were differences. This Queen had a crown on her head and her attitude was more regal than Medb's. Her eyes and body were more guarded and Cathbad reckoned that she wasn't as generous with her smiles. Also, the animals surrounding her were different. There were three leopards at her feet, in various states of rest. The druid guessed that these were the cats that once guarded the cave that they had come through. On her left shoulder was the white crow that had led them here. And in her lap was a pair of foxes, watching everything intently.

The two men stood to one side as the Queen discussed some business with a couple of her ministers. After she had dismissed them she seemed to look directly at the two mortals for a while before saying, 'I can see you.'

They looked at each other.

'Don't be surprised. I have the eyes of a hawk.'

'Uh, Queen Medb said to say hello,' Cathbad said.

'Did she now? I take it you've come through Oweyna-gat?'

'Yes, Queen.'

'And what do you think of my city?'

'Very beautiful, Queen.'

'Thank you, druid. So, why are you here? I'm sure you haven't come all this way to give regards from Medb.'

'No, we've come to reclaim a soul you acquired recently. That of Cú Chulainn of Emain Macha,' Cathbad said.

'One of my prize possessions. And why should I give him up to you?'

'Because, Queen, this is not his destiny. His destiny is to die in battle.'

'Here in the Otherworld there is no destiny, druid. That is the province of mortals only.'

'But he doesn't belong here. He said it to us himself. He yearns to return to the mortal realm.'

'Many souls do. And in time he may return. In a different form. But for now, he stays with me.'

'That's cruelty!' Laeg exclaimed. Cathbad elbowed and shushed him.

'If you let him return and he dies a noble death, then surely he will make a greater possession.'

'Nobody dies twice,' the Queen said. 'It's against the rules.'

'Cú Chulainn could,' Laeg said.

'You are the ruler here, Queen, are you not?' Cathbad said.

'Yes. I am.'

'Then if anyone can break the rules, it's you.'

'Ok, saying I do break the rules and send him back. What would you give me in return?"

Cathbad gave a long sigh and said, 'I would give you myself. I would give you my body and my soul.'

'Cathbad! What –'

'Keep quiet, Laeg,' the druid snapped. 'This is something you do not possess, Queen. A mortal. And when I die, I'll be yours for evermore.'

'Hmmm. This does sound interesting,' the Queen said.

'I have a lot to offer. Stories and knowledge. A lifetime's worth. I could be useful to you.'

'But you have no fame.'

'Fame is overrated, Queen. Knowledge is far more preferable. In my book.'

'And what about this young man who accompanies you? Do I get him as well?'

'Ah, Queen. He is only Cú Chulainn's charioteer. You don't want him.'

'Thanks,' Laeg said, glumly.

'Besides, he is needed to bring Cú Chulainn's soul back to the mortal realm.'

The Queen sighed deeply and looked at the two questers for a long time, in silence. 'I won't lie to you. This offer interests me,' she said. 'But I need some time alone. To think about it. Please wait outside for a few minutes while I decide.'

Outside, there was a wooden bench that was placed against one of the ivied walls of the castle. They sat down here to await the Queen's decision. They could see Cú Chulainn. He was still seated on the rock but he had turned around to watch the castle for any developments.

'What are you up to, Cathbad? Are you crazy?' Laeg said. He looked at the druid with rounded eyes.

'You heard what I said. I'm offering my body and soul for the safe return of Cú Chulainn.'

'Surely there must be another way.'

'If there is, I don't know about it.'

'But you can't just throw away your life like this!'

'Yes, I can, boy. It is mine to throw away.'

Laeg shook his head but couldn't find any more words to say.

'All my life I've been a selfish person. It's time to give something back,' the druid said.

'That's not true! You are needed in Emain Macha! Who is going to act as druid?'

'It is a selfish occupation, Laeg. I get to do pretty much what I want. It's made me a little crazy, after all these years. As for who is going to take my place, I've already discussed it with Feargus. He has agreed to take on and train the next druid of Emain Macha. There are already some youngsters who have expressed an interested in the role.'

'But that would mean you were planning this all along!' Laeg said.

'Not planning, Laeg. Just preparing. For the worst.'

'Why didn't you tell me?'

'Because I didn't know how it would all pan out. Look at him. It's so strange to see him like this.' Cú Chulainn had stood up and stepped closer to the castle. Now he was standing near the two travellers. He stood with his weight shifted on one leg, like Michelangelo's David. 'I should have been a better grandfather to him, Laeg. I should have watched out for him.'

'That may be so. But it doesn't mean you have to give your life for him.'

'I'm an old man, Laeg. He is just a kid. I belong here, he doesn't. That is the natural order of things. Besides, I think I could get to like life in these parts. It might be a good place to spend my final years.'

'You still have a long way to go, Cathbad.'

'Perhaps. But why spend it locked it away in my house, high on glamberries? I think I'd prefer to be somewhere I am wanted.'

Laeg sighed and said, 'it's your decision, druid. It's your decision.'

They fell into silence, awaiting the call to return to the throne room. As they did so, they watched the ghost of Cú Chulainn. Cathbad was right. It was strange seeing him like this. Would they ever see the old Cú Chulainn again? He had been through so much these last couple of weeks and he still had much to do, if the Queen agreed to Cathbad's deal.

'Wasted years,' Laeg said.

'Hmmm?'

'You said that if you don't change at least once in your life, you've wasted it.'

'Ah, hmm. Did I?' the druid said, looking pleased at being quoted.

'You're a wise man, Cathbad. Crazy as a bat, but wise. It's been good getting to know you. I'm going to miss you.'

'And I you, young man. You are a loyal friend to come all this way with me. I hope Cú Chulainn appreciates this when he returns.'

At this point, the Queen called them back into the throne room. Her voice was soft but it carried far, as if being sustained by some magic.

The two men stood before her again. She had taken the crown off her head and it rested in her lap. Her eyes glowed with pleasure. She even managed a small but benign smile. The three leopards at her feet were now alert. They watched the questers in a quiet, predatory way.

'I've thought about your offer and I've decided to take you up on it. Your body and soul for the body and soul of Cú Chulainn.'

Laeg looked at the druid and smiled triumphantly but Cathbad just nodded his head at the Queen, in quiet approval.

'How can we bring back the Hound in both body and soul, great Queen? I must admit this question has vexed me greatly,' the druid said.

'It is easy, druid,' the Queen said. She looked down at the crown in her lap, then she removed a single sapphire gemstone from its base. 'Here,' she said and held it out for Cathbad to take. The old man hesitated, looking at the leopards. 'Don't worry about them, Cathbad. They do what I tell them to.' As he accepted the stone, the Queen said, 'the soul of Cú Chulainn is contained in that jewel. If his body is still extant, you must remove his left eye and replace it with the stone. If he has been cremated, you'll have to find another host for him. Either way, the stone will bring your Hound back to life.'

'Are you serious?' Laeg said.

'Yes, young man.'

'Won't it look a little strange?'

'Yes, it might mar his beauty a little.'

Cathbad looked at the gemstone in his hand. 'Hmmm. It does make sense, Laeg. They say that the eyes are the window to the soul.'

'Cú Chulainn had brown eyes,' the young man pointed out.

'So?' the druid said.

'What kind of a strange soul has one brown eye and one blue?'

'He might get a few odd looks but people will accept it, in time.'

The Queen clapped her hands once, loudly, and said, 'very well. The deal is done. I expect you two will want to say your farewells.' She stood up and walked away from the throne, stately, carrying the crown in one nonchalant hand. The leopards followed her soundlessly. In this way she left the room.

Cathbad handed the sapphire stone to Laeg.

'Keep it safe, Laeg. It's best if you go straight back to Emain Macha when you leave the cave. We don't want it falling into the wrong hands. In fact, don't tell anyone, even in Emain Macha. Not until you've performed the operation.'

'But how will I do it?'

'Easy. Just gouge the eye out and replace it with the stone.'

Laeg grimaced a little at this. 'I don't know if I can do that, Cathbad.'

'Here. Take this,' Cathbad said and produced a small knife from a pocket of his robe. 'It should make it easier. Oh, and I almost forgot. Take this, too.' The druid produced a small vial and handed it to Laeg. 'The aphrodisiac. For the Bull,' Cathbad said by way of explanation.

'I wish you were coming with me.'

'Me too, Laeg. Me too. I'm sorry but this is the best I can do. And when Cú Chulainn returns, you must tell him this, as well. I'm sorry! I'm so damn sorry!'

Cathbad's eyes began to well up. Laeg made to embrace him but something in the druid's look made him hesitate.

'This is a noble act, Cathbad. And I'll make sure no one forgets it.'

'Yes, yes. Good lad. Go on now. Off with you.'

And so Laeg turned around and left the castle.

Outside, the ghost of Cú Chulainn still hung around, waiting for news. It suddenly occurred to Laeg that the Queen might have cheated them. That the stone he now possessed contained nothing beyond its beautiful sapphire substance. Unfortunately, there was no way of telling. So, he had to crush the thought and trust the Queen.

Laeg found that the journey back to the mortal realm was a lot easier. The only real encounter he had was with the strange woman and the uillean piper, at threshold to the Otherworld.

The piper still sat on the rock but he was silent. And the woman still stood behind him in her crimson robe. They looked at Laeg intently as he entered the cave.

'Where is he?' the woman said slowly, and again there was that undercurrent of emotion that made her voice quaver a little and made Laeg afraid.

Laeg produced the sapphire and held it between thumb and forefinger. He explained about the deal they had made with the Queen.

'I see. Then you mustn't fail in your task, Laeg,' the woman said, and the young man was relieved to hear the satisfaction in her voice.

'I won't.'

'You are going to miss your druid friend, yes?'

'Yes. I feel like I had only started to get to know him,' Laeg said. For some reason, this woman made him want to speak the truth.

'There are many such turns in life, Laeg. You must just follow them and see where they take you.' As if on cue, the piper started up again. It was a lively music in a major key. Laeg took this as a sign that he was being dismissed. But before he left them, he took one last look at the woman and she smiled serenely at him.

He left the room and entered the corridor which led back to Oweynagat. For a long time, he heard the music of the piper following him, but gradually getting fainter and fainter as he went deeper.

The luminescent designs on the walls had not the power they formally had. And they too gradually got fainter until he was enveloped in pitch dark. The way home was always easier, the young man reflected. Probably because you knew what to expect. But he wasn't home yet. The Hound awaited him. There was some strange magic to perform. And he had absolutely no idea what was waiting for him. He cursed inwardly. This was druid's work. Not suitable for a charioteer. But he did have one thing: he was Cú Chulainn's best friend. And that might count for something.

When at last he emerged into daylight, his eyes throbbed with pain but he couldn't help smiling. He had made it! He took the sapphire stone out of his pocket and held it up to the light. Then, suddenly, he felt slightly ridiculous. Standing there in his vagabond's rags, holding a stone that he thought contained the soul of his best friend.

Maybe it had all been a dream. Or some kind of illusion. If so, where was Cathbad? He remembered the sacrifice the druid had made and this made him resolute. He would see this to the end. Even if it was some kind of mad delusion.

'What's that you've got there?' a voice said. Laeg looked up to see Feargus standing on the forest floor above him. He went up the incline until he stood face to face with the druid. 'Tell me everything,' he said, and so Laeg did.

When he had told Feargus everything, the druid continued to look at him in silence for a moment before turning his eyes away into the middle distance and nodding his head.

'He said you had made an agreement? About training our next druid?'

'Aye. Just tell Conchobar to send the lad to me when he's decided on who it should be.'

'Do you think he'll be ok?' Laeg said.

'Who? Cathbad? O, I'm sure he will. It won't be long before he's driving everyone mad, haha. I'll miss him though. He was a good man and a good friend. I knew him when he was a young fellow, you know. The things we got up to, together! Yes. Maybe I'll tell you about it sometime. But for now, let's get you blindfolded and away on your way home.

'Is it absolutely necessary?'

'You know it is, Laeg,' the druid said and proceeded to tie the silken scarf around the young man's head.

'Now, put your hand on my shoulder and follow me.'

VI

Cú Chulainn Returns

How did Laeg bring back Cú Chulainn and what transpired?

It is soon told.

Laeg encountered hardly anyone on his way back to Emain Macha and those people he did pass by gave him no notice at all. In fact, they seemed to look straight through him as if he were a ghost. Sometimes he couldn't help wondering if the Queen had taken his soul too, but he knew that it was probably just the rags he wore.

Luckily, the good weather persisted, so he kept dry and warm. Sometimes, when he sat at the fire in the evening, he would take out the silver apple the woman in the crimson robe had given him. It was so handsome! Then he would take out the sapphire that contained the soul of Cú Chulainn. It was so beautiful! So multi-faceted! It seemed that his travels had made him a rich man. He could exchange these treasures for a farm and settle down for the rest of his life, if he wanted to. But nothing would be worth more than having his friend back.

Then he would think of the gruesome work ahead. Replacing the dead man's eye with the jewel. It almost made him shudder to think of it. And he worried about what he was bringing back to life. It was so unnatural! What if he brought back something bad? Something evil? But there was no turning back now. Cathbad had sacrificed his life for this jewel. All he could do was perform the gruesome business and hope that Cú Chulainn's spirit was strong enough to make the journey back to the world of the living, pure and untainted. He was going to be changed, that was for sure. But changed like a man who has gone away from home for a long time, Laeg hoped. And sure wasn't he changed, himself? He had travelled across the country and gone to the heart of the Otherworld to speak with the Queen who held dominion over it. He had seen artwork and heard music that was so powerful, it awoke in him feelings he didn't know he had. And he had seen buildings of a grandeur and beauty that was unknown in Emain Macha or anywhere in the land.

The only real encounter he had was with a band of thieves, about halfway along his journey. It was midday and he strolled through the trees in good spirits. For the first time in a very long while he began to whistle a tune. The closer he got to home, the more his mood lightened, it seemed.

'What are you so pleased about, tramp?' a gravelly voice said. Three men came out from the trees and stopped him in his tracks. They were ruddy and scar faced, except for the young man who had spoken, who was eminently handsome and looked like he knew it, too. All three had daggers raised. Laeg looked at them, thinking about what to say.

'Well?' the leader said.

'Nothing much. It's just a nice day is all,' Laeg said.

'I don't believe you. You sound like a man who has just come into some luck. Want to share it with us, tramp?'

'I've nothing I want to share with you, thief,' Laeg said and smiled thinly at the man.

'Ok. Search him, boys. And be quick about it.'

'Ok. Hold it. Hold it,' Laeg said. 'I'll show you what I have. Here.' He produced the silver apple and the sapphire, one in each hand. The leader of the band of thieves looked at them. His face slackened and his eyes turned soft.

'What are they?' he said, distantly.

Laeg looked the man in the eye and said, 'the apple I got from the Otherworld while I was looking for the soul of a dead friend. The sapphire I got from the Queen of that realm. It contains the soul of said friend. I must go to the place where his mortal remains are and replace his left eye with it, in order to resurrect him.' Then Laeg smiled at the man and he put all the craziness he could muster into that smile. The man started to laugh. His eyes hardened again but there was more than a hint of fear in them.

155

'You're crazy,' he said.

'O, you don't know the half of it,' Laeg said and started to laugh too.

'Go on,' the man ordered. 'Leave these parts and whatever you do, don't come back.'

Laeg stopped laughing but he continued to smile at the man in that thin, lunatic way. Then, he looked at the other two thieves. They turned their faces away, unable to meet his eye. So, he put away the treasures and continued on his path homeward.

Cú Chulainn's barrow was very large, as befitted a warrior of his status. It was also some distance away from the vicinity of Emain Macha which suited Laeg as he didn't want anyone interfering in the work he had to do. The site basically consisted of a great mound of stones with an entrance at ground level. It was like an inversion of the cave of Oweynagat in Cruachan. The only real difficulty Laeg anticipated was the moving of the stone that blocked off the entrance.

But, as it turned out, there was no need to worry about this – someone had already moved the entrance stone aside, giving free ingress to the tomb. So, one worry was replaced by another: what if the tomb had been raided? What if Cú Chulainn's body had been desecrated? For he had made many enemies in his time. And what if the invaders were still inside? What had seemed like a gruesome business could turn even more nasty and bloody.

He approached the entrance carefully, quietly, obliquely. When he reached it, he stopped and listened for a long time but there were no sounds coming from it. Eventually, satisfied that there was nobody in the barrow, he entered it.

The smell of decay was powerful, but he continued into the heart of the tomb, unfazed.

What he found surprised even him. There was no body! The slab on which the Hound had lain was bare!

Laeg looked about him in disbelief. All he saw were shadows. And in his mind too there were only shadows. Who, in their right mind, would want to steal a corpse? What purpose would it serve? Even if it was the corpse of the greatest warrior who ever lived, it was still a corpse. Gone, like all of us, to death the leveller.

Then a voice came from the shadows. 'I've been waiting for you, Laeg,' it said. It was a watery voice, like someone trying to speak and gargle at the same time.

'Who are you?'

'Look at me, Laeg. Look into the shadows,' the voice said.

Laeg tried to pierce the gloom with his eyes. 'I can't. I...' Then he could make out a form sitting nonchalantly on a rock in a corner of the tomb. 'Cú Chulainn? Is that you?'

'That depends, doesn't it? On who or what is Cú Chulainn?'

'I don't understand...'

'Well, am I Cú Chulainn? Or is Cú Chulainn contained in that jewel you plan to disfigure me with?'

'I don't know…'

'You weren't expecting this, were you? You weren't expecting me to be alive?'

'I…'

'You thought I would make it easy for you. That I would just lie down and let you take out my eye and stick a bloody stone into my skull. Well, Laeg, I'm sorry but I won't give in that easily.'

'Let me at least tell you what happened, Hound.'

'You don't need to. I know enough.'

'She said that it contained your soul. The sapphire,' Laeg said.

'And you trust her? You believe her?'

'Yes. She's the Queen of the Otherworld. The spirit realm.'

'Ghosts. Ghosts. Nothing more than ghosts. Maybe all she wants is to mar my beauty. Maybe she is jealous. Did that ever cross your mind?'

'But I don't understand. You died. You shouldn't be here, talking to me.'

'Is that right? Maybe I just went to sleep. And now I've awoken.'

'But I saw your spirit. In the Otherworld.'

'And did you talk to me?'

'No, I couldn't. I tried to…'

'See? That was no soul. Just a ghost. An illusion. And that sapphire you have is no more than a pretty stone. The truth is there is no soul, Laeg. But even if there was one, it's a bit overrated. Don't you think?'

'I don't believe you,' Laeg said.

'I'm here, aren't I?'

'You're not Cú Chulainn. Wherever you came from.'

'Is that right?'

'Yes. Cú Chulainn was a good man. You are not. You are rotten. A talking corpse.'

'O dear. I was hoping I might be able to convince you by argument but it seems that will not be the case.' The creature tossed something at Laeg. The young man caught it. It was a sword. 'Luckily they buried me with two of these,' it said and produced another from its sheath. 'Now, if you still intend to go ahead with this business, you'll have to fight me first.'

'I'm not going to fight you,' Laeg said.

'Why not?'

'Because you might be a corpse but you are the corpse of my best friend, damn you.'

'Ah, see. Now you are approaching sense. I am your best friend. Is it so hard to accept that?'

'You're an empty vessel. And I intend to fill you.'

'So, you are going to fight me?'

Laeg answered with silence.

'Are you sure you want to? You know I'm good.'

'No. There is no goodness in you,' Laeg said. 'Let me put the stone into you. Let me bring Cú Chulainn back to life.

What kind of existence will you have if I don't? Skulking around here. Decaying into nothingness.'

'Dying's not so bad, Laeg. An end to it all. Extinction. I mean, who wants to live forever?'

'I've been to the Otherworld and I intend to return some-day. Don't knock it 'til you've tried it.'

'You poor, deluded fool. I'll send you on your way. So, you can see for yourself. There is no Otherworld. No spirit realm. It's all in your imagination.'

'Maybe. Maybe the soul resides in the imagination. Did that thought ever enter your head?'

'Clever. Your wits have improved. But can you outwit my sword?' The creature stood up and approached Laeg, slowly, deliberately. 'Outside,' it said.

Laeg backed away until they were both standing outside the mound. The corpse of Cú Chulainn didn't give him much time for inspection. All he could make out was a death-pale face with red rimmed eyes, and an expression of rage that was beyond anything Laeg had ever witnessed. Then the creature was all over him. Before he knew what was happening, the creature had disarmed him and had him lying supine on the ground.

'You know my talent, Laeg. You know I'm a killing ma-chine. I never had a soul. So, why fight me?'

'You were more than that. You were a great guy. I know because I was your best friend.'

The creature made to cleave Laeg but the young man managed to roll out of the way. He stood up and faced the corpse again. He pulled the knife Cathbad had given him out from his rags and looked at it. He shook his head. It was no match for the sword of Cú Chulainn but he had nothing else to fight with, so he raised it at the creature. Cú Chulainn's corpse laughed and kicked it out of his hand.

He was now almost completely defenceless. He felt like running away but he knew that this creature would be on him in seconds. The only defence he had were words.

'Cathbad gave his life for you. Did you know that?' Laeg said.

'That madman! If he wanted to throw away his life, that was his choice. Nothing to do with me.'

'He was your grandfather.'

'He told you that?'

'Yes. He said to say he was sorry. That this was the best he could do. I don't know why I'm telling you this. His words are wasted on you.'

'That's right. I'm a killing machine. I never had a god-damned soul.'

'Yes you did.'

The creature hawked and spat onto the ground beside him.

Sensing that he was getting somewhere, Laeg said, 'don't you at least want to take a look at it?'

'A look at what?' the creature gargled.

'Your soul.'

Cú Chulainn's corpse grinned and said, 'alright. Show it to me. I could do with a laugh.'

So, Laeg produced the sapphire from his rags and held it up between the thumb and forefinger of his right hand. The creature approached. At first it only sneered but this was soon replaced by a frown and what looked almost like a smile. 'It is pretty. I'll give you that,' it said.

'Come closer. See how it reflects the light. It's a beauty,' Laeg said.

And the creature obeyed. Its face softened, just like that of the thief. When it was a few inches from the stone, it cocked its head. It looked like it was about to say something but Laeg didn't give it a chance. He closed his hand around the jewel, making a fist, drew it back and then punched the creature, right in the centre of its forehead. There was an explosion of power from the stone and the creature fell down on its back, unconscious. Laeg grabbed the knife Cathbad had given him and went to work on the creature immediately, not wanting to waste any time.

The operation went smoothly and easily. He simply levered the creature's left eye out with the knife and then replaced it with the sapphire. He had to use a small amount of force to push it home. When he had finished, he looked at his handiwork. Not too bad, he reflected. A bit like a pirate. But it still remained to be seen whether the procedure was a success or not.

'Cú Chulainn?' he said. There was no response. 'Cú Chulainn?' he repeated, shaking his friend's shoulder. There was still nothing. Laeg sighed and said, 'you better wake up soon, Hound. The amount of trouble we went to –'

Cú Chulainn opened his remaining eye wide and took a deep, deep breath, like someone who has been underwater for a long time. Then he sat up, panting and looking around him. 'Laeg?' he said, at last.

'Yes. It's me,' his friend said.

'My eye. What happened to my eye?'

'I'm sorry, Cú. I had to take it out. To get you back.'

'Why are you dressed in rags?'

Laeg laughed and said, 'all will soon be told. In the meantime, just breathe the air again. It's good to have you back.'

When Laeg and Cú Chulainn walked through the streets of Emain Macha again, they received some strange looks. People had found it hard to accept the fact that the Hound had died and now they found it even harder to accept that he had returned. Of course, the sapphire in his eye socket didn't help things. People looked at it with suspicion and even a little disgust.

But there was no denying that Cú Chulainn was a changed man. This change registered in his silence more than anything else he did. He just didn't talk as much as he used to. At first, Laeg resented this a little but he soon found himself accepting it. He remembered what Cathbad had said

163

about change. If it didn't happen at least once, you've wasted your life. Yes, the Hound had changed but Laeg loved him anyway.

Emer, however, was another story. It was hard for her to accept that Cú Chulainn had returned. She had grieved for him. She had keened at his tomb. She had come to terms with his loss and now he was back again. It was all so confusing for her. But she also was frustrated by how changed he was. She simply couldn't reach him anymore. He wouldn't talk to her. And this drove her a little insane. Unlike Laeg, she just couldn't get over it. And so, they separated.

The Hound went to live in Cathbad's old house. Laeg had told him about the druid's sacrifice and Cú Chulainn had answered him with a weary, troubled silence. Soon after, though, he publicly acknowledged that Cathbad was his grandfather. However, to the people of Emain Macha, he was now considered as strange as Cathbad had been and that was the only reason why he should inherit the house. It was nothing to do with kinship.

Not long after their return to the village, Laeg paid a visit to Conchobar in his royal house. He handed him the vial that Medb had given to Cathbad and explained its purpose.

'Cathbad saw it as another sign that peace is on the way.'

'Cathbad was an optimist,' the King said.

'No, he was a pacifist. And I'm starting to believe he was right to be so.'

Conchobar gave a perfunctory nod and looked at the vial. He unplugged it and was about to take a sniff when Laeg said, 'I wouldn't do that if I was you.' The King looked at him for a few seconds and then decided it was best not to defy Laeg, as defying him was the same as defying Medb and he was wise enough not to do that.

'It is a good gesture and it will be returned,' Conchobar said.

'Very good, King. And don't forget that her druid, Fear-gus, agreed with Cathbad to take on and train his successor,' Laeg said.

'Yes. That too will be answered. If the great heifer produces a bull-calf, I will make a gift of it to Medb. How is that?'

'Excellent, King! Have you decided on who will be the next druid?'

'Yes, young Dathí Suibhne wants the role. I will send him to Cruachan with my thanks and my promise very soon.'

Laeg grinned at this. Conchobar was glad to see that the blonde young man hadn't changed entirely.

'How is the Hound?' the King asked.

'Fine, I guess. I don't see him much. No one does.'

'I'm still waiting for him to visit me, Laeg. I know it must be hard for him but it really is disrespectful,' Conchobar said.

'Give him more time, Conchobar. I think he deserves it.'

'Yes. You're right. He does. But he doesn't have to tell me everything. I just want to see him and ask him if he is ok. He is as much a friend to me as he is a subject.'

'I'll talk to him. He doesn't mean any disrespect. He just doesn't like reliving what he went through.'

'He doesn't have to. I just want to ask him about his well-being and what he is going to do with himself. If there is a permanent peace on the cards, like you say there is, he's going to need a new occupation. And so will you, come to think of it.'

'Plenty of time, Conchobar. Plenty of time to think about that. Our immediate concern should be the finding of the Heifer and the Brown Bull and the bringing of them together. Remember your promise. The bull-calf born of their union will be the seal of a permanent peace between Emain Macha and Rathcruachan.'

'Ok, I'll get some men on it. It's a pity Cathbad isn't here to help out. He had a way with the Brown Bull.'

'Yes, he was gentle underneath it all. Do you think young Dathi will be able to fill his boots?'

'Who knows? The lad certainly has potential. If he wants it badly enough then maybe in time...?'

'You know, Cú Chulainn said to me there will come a time when druids are no longer needed. And that it's not far from now,' Laeg said.

'Did he? I find that hard to imagine.'

'You can imagine peace, can't you?'

'Yes, I suppose so.'

'There you go. Maybe that's all it takes. Maybe to imagine is to make real.'

'You're in speculative mood today, young Laeg.'

'Yeah, I know, I've a lot on my mind.'

'You've changed, too. Maybe not as much as the Hound but you have.'

Laeg nodded and smiled. 'You remind me of Cathbad, something he said.'

'I wish he was still around. I wish I had gotten to know him as well as you did,' Conchobar said.

'Just be happy for him. He gave up his life knowing that he hadn't wasted it.'

'Yes. That is something. Now let's get on to this other business. We have a wedding to plan!'

A wise man once said that to remember everything is a form of madness. If that was the case then Cú Chulainn was mad beyond recall.

For he remembered everything: floating on the sea, the voices of the fire, the journey with Socrates, training with Merlin, going to Troy, even his time in the Otherworld. This last recollection came only in flashes but he remembered enough to feel sad when he thought about it. For he did not belong there in the Otherworld. And now, it seemed, he did not belong in Emain Macha either. So, where did that leave him? But what troubled and saddened him the most was the knowledge that Cathbad had sacrificed his life for him. He had given up his body and soul for this? So that his grandson could walk the streets of Emain Macha and be met with looks of fear, suspicion and disgust everywhere he went? So that he could alienate his wife, his friends, even his King? He had once been too embarrassed to acknowledge that the druid was his grandfather. Now, he felt unworthy and ashamed of himself.

The only person he would talk to was Laeg. They had been best friends and they had renewed their bond, especially after Laeg had brought him back to life. They talked about Cathbad's last days much of the time. According to Laeg, the druid had shown a different side to his personality. A wiser, gentler side. And Cú Chulainn found himself a little envious of Laeg for having known this.

Yes, he would talk to Laeg, as long as it wasn't about what he had gone through. He just couldn't do that. It was obvious that the young man had quite a story to tell, himself, and he had no trouble telling it but the Hound just couldn't reciprocate. Only he would ever know what he went through and that was the simple truth of it.

So, it was with a heavy heart and mind that the Hound waited for Laeg to join him on the bank of the river, one evening. It was a gorgeous, mellow Autumn nightfall: the birds in the trees sang ecstatically, the air was sweet and the mead was good. All these things conspired to cheer him up but they failed. He just stared into the shadows on the other side of the quiet river.

Laeg had almost reached him by the time he noticed the blonde young man approaching. He grinned his trademark grin and he had his mead horn out almost before he sat down beside the Hound. After taking a deep draught, he looked at Cú Chulainn and said, 'good news! The Heifer is pregnant!'

'Is that right?' the Hound said, distantly.

'Well, don't sound too enthusiastic.'

'I'm sorry, Laeg. It's just that that heifer got me into a lot of trouble.'

'No use crying over spilt milk, is there? No pun intended.'

'No. There isn't,' the Hound said. He continued to look into shadows on the bank opposite.

'Don't you know what this means?' Laeg said, a little exasperated.

'Yeah, I know. If it's a bull-calf, Conchobar plans to make a gift of it to Medb. But what if it isn't?'

'It'll be a bull-calf.'

'Who says so?' the Hound said.

'Destiny says so.'

'And you think it will lead to a permanent peace?'

'Yes. And it's what Cathbad believed, too.' Cú Chulainn gave him a warning look and Laeg swiftly changed the subject. 'So, it looks like young Dathi is going to be the next druid. He will be leaving for Cruachan in a couple of days-time.'

'Good for him.'

'Have you given any thought about what you intend to do? Now that there will be peace?' Laeg said.

Cú Chulainn just shook his head and stared at his hands. 'I was born to kill people, Laeg. There is no place for me in a civilised society.'

'Come on, Cú. You know better than that. You must give something a try. You're still young. There is time.'

'Time to waste.'

'No. Time to live. Time to grow.'

'Destiny says otherwise, Laeg. I must die young. In bat-tle.'

'But you've already done that, Cú! You died on the plain at Troy! You are free of that curse!'

The Hound continued to look at his hands.

'Or are you afraid?'

'Afraid of what?' Cú Chulainn said, giving him a black look.

'To live without destiny. To be free.'

There was a silence. A plop came from the slow river.

'It's all I've ever known, Laeg.'

'Do you think you are the only one? The only person to have gone through what you have gone through?'

'What are you talking about?'

'Your journey. Your quest for knowledge.'

'I don't want to go there, Laeg.'

'You know, it happens to all of us. Sorry to disappoint you but it does.'

Cú Chulainn shook his head but remained silent.

'You learned what we all learn, didn't you? You learned that the soul is free.'

'No, I didn't.'

'Yes, you did. You know you wouldn't have been able to come back if it wasn't.'

'I was her prisoner, Laeg.'

'I know. I was there. I saw you. I saw how unhappy you were. And the reason you were so unhappy was that you resented being kept. Like anyone would.'

'But if there is no place for me in the Otherworld...?'

'You know, the Otherworld is a pretty materialistic place. I noticed that when I went there. Maybe it's not the destination of all souls, after all. Maybe it's just a brief resting place. Before we go on. You know, like a halfway house?'

'Interesting speculation,' the Hound said. 'So where do we go from there?'

'No one knows. But wherever it is I'll bet that it's free. That it's a free country.'

Cú Chulainn looked at his hands again. They were worn and battle-scarred. He didn't know what to say.

'So, now that you know you are free, what are you going do about it? Are you going to stay shut away in your house on the edge of town for the rest of your years or are you going to go out there and embrace it and do something?'

'When did you get so wise?' Cú Chulainn said and couldn't help smiling a little.

'I had some help. From a friend.'

The Hound nodded and they shared another silence.

'This place is so beautiful at this time,' the Hound said, eventually. 'I mean, sitting here, talking and drinking with you. In the good weather. It makes me so happy. It really does. I wish I could express it in words or music. But I can't. I'm just not creative.'

'Sometimes the desire to create is enough,' Laeg said.

'No. Thanks for saying that but…I think I'd like to get a hurling team together. You know how good I am with a ball and stick. I think I could make the greatest hurling team in Ireland.'

'Some people would disagree with you there but, yes, I think that's a great idea, Hound.'

'What about yourself?'

'Well, I was thinking of becoming a cook. You know I'm good at multi-tasking. And you've tried my legendary fry-ups.'

'Very good, Laeg. I think you'd make a fine cook.'

'I'll miss the old partnership though. You and me in the chariot. Scaring the hell out of everyone.'

'Yes, when we were good, we were very good.'

'The best,' Laeg said. 'So, when are you going to see Conchobar?'

The Hound sighed and shook his head. 'Someday.'

'You can't keep putting it off. He is your King. He wants to see you. What are you afraid of?'

'I guess I just don't want to be the Warped One anymore. And that's all I'll ever be to him.'

'That's not true, Hound. He is also your friend.'

'He's a king, Laeg. And I'm his subject. It's a power relation. No more. He has the power. And now that Cathbad is gone, he has more power than ever. But you know what? I think I *will* visit him. Just to look him in the eye and tell him that he doesn't own me anymore. That I'm no longer his weapon.'

'If that's what you need to do,' Laeg said. 'But be careful.'

'I will. I know him well enough.'

'But do you know yourself?'

'Ok, enough of these clever exchanges. Let's just shut up and enjoy the peace for a moment,' the Hound said.

And so they did.

On the far bank something stirred the shadows. It was a rat, creeping softly.

'You know, there are places in India where rats are considered sacred,' Laeg said.

'Is that right?' the Hound replied.

'See? You think you know everything and then this rat comes along to spoil it.'

173

'They're not so bad. He doesn't mean any harm. He's gone now, anyway. Had his moment.'

'A bit like us humans,' Laeg said.

The night continued to fall but the conversation turned lighter. They drank and conversed like it was the old days, when they were as new gods – happy, immortal and free. And the birds and the breeze carried memories. And ghosts and shadows stirred across the water. And Time loitered nonchalantly and made them its solemn promises, to which they gave silent heed.

Yes, the night continued to fall. And the world to fade. And their hearts to sing. And it was all anyone could hope for and they were all anyone could hope to be.

David Jordan lives and works out of Cork, Ireland. He has an MA in English.

He blogs at shadowoftheglen.wordpress.com